Jennifer Sinclair

Fiery Dunes

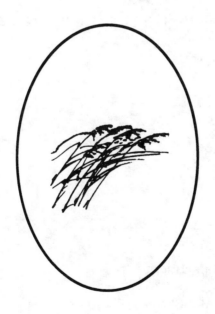

Lorelei Publications

This book is a work of fiction. Names, characters, places, and incidents are either products of the author's imagination or are used fictitiously. Any resemblance to actual events or locales or persons, living or dead, is purely coincidental.

Library of Congress Card Catalog Number: 95-95000

ISBN 1-57502-051-3

Printed in the USA by

*M*ORRIS
PUBLISHING

3212 E. Hwy 30
Kearney, NE 68847
800-650-7888

Lorelei Publications
Mail Order Department
P.O. Box 3774
Gulf Shores, AL 36547-3774

DEDICATION

For Hays and Mary Anne Tapia and
Gerald and Mib Kidd,
dearest friends who embody the finest Old South traditions
with style and grace

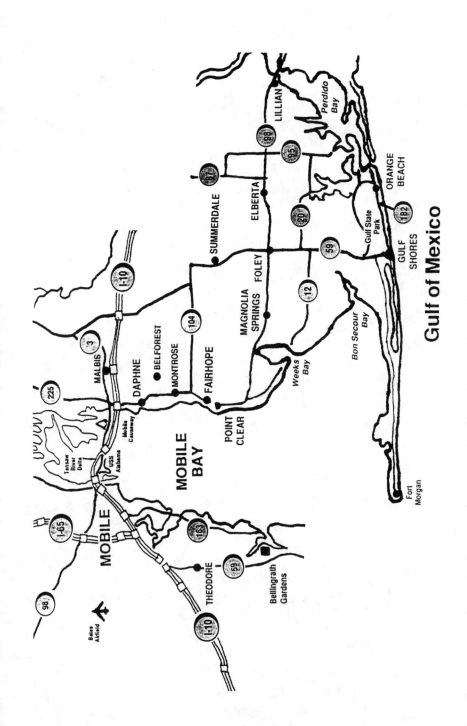

CHAPTER 1

Devastated and heartsick, Anne paced along the deserted beach. All she'd ever wanted was about to become a memory and she felt so trapped, so alone.

She thought about regaining control of her destiny, if only the economy would improve, if--if only. She shook her head and walked on, thinking, that's the future and this is now. I've got to go on, that's all there is to it, the bottom line.

As head of Livingston Enterprises, she now faced her final duty. The time had come for her to sign over the last of her family's holdings in the healthcare franchise she unwittingly had brought to the attention of corporate raiders.

That thought turned her stomach and tore at her heart. How unfair that her success had led to her company's demise. Powerless to defend against deep pockets and vicious rumors, she'd watched Livingston Enterprises become acquisition fodder.

When talk of insider shenanigans had first surfaced, she'd refused to assign blame to those she'd trusted. She'd thought she could stop the insanity before things got out of control, but that hadn't happened.

That was when she'd faced the facts, as distressing as they were, and determined she'd find the strength to start over, somehow, someway.

Stooping to pick up a sand dollar, Anne paused to admire the fragile gift from the sea. So delicate and perfect. She slipped it into her jacket pocket and continued her walk by the water's edge. Closing her eyes, she concentrated on listening to the calming call of the Gulf. She felt renewed, almost hopeful.

Anne climbed a high dune and turned for one last look at the water. Peace washed over her and strength filled her soul.

Reluctantly, she returned to her car. As she drove across the Bay to Mobile, she mentally prepared herself for the conference meeting she'd set for 9:00 a.m. the next day. I can handle it, she thought, then she corrected herself-- no, there's no "can" to it, I "will" handle it. That was her final plan.

* * * * *

"Stupid alarm! Stop!! Now!!!" Anne commanded. She wadded up her pillow and buried her head underneath its doubled fold.

The alarm roared unmercifully until Anne silenced it with a heavy-handed swat. Grumbling about rude awakenings, fretful sleep, and jangled nerves, she tossed off her covers and rolled out of bed.

Peeking through the curtains, she hoped to catch a glimpse of a promising daybreak. Cloudy darkness stared back. Anne thought how fitting a greeting for what seemed predestined to become the gloomiest day of her life.

She watched her cat, Bella, yawn and stretch lazily across her comforter. "Maybe I should join you and call in sick," Anne said, somewhat envious of Bella's peaceful state. Gently scratching underneath Bella's chin, she added, "But that wouldn't be right, would it?"

In response, Bella covered her head with her paws.

"Okay, I get the message. I'm out of here."

Anne walked to her closet and reached inside. Selecting a grey pinstripe suit, white blouse, and black pumps, she sighed as she pictured herself in the boardroom on the top floor of the Livingston Centre.

"Definitely austere. A perfect match for today's agenda," she said as she dressed in front of the mirror she'd attached to her closet door. Then she fastened her hair in a sensible knot at the nape of her neck and commented dryly, "Strictly business, yes indeed, here I go."

Turning away from her picture perfect image, she bumped against her dresser that was wedged into the corner of her compact dressing room. A hatbox she used for ribbons and scarves hit the floor with a bang.

Curious, Bella pounced on the tangle of silk and grosgrain. She pawed at a red headband Anne had forgotten she owned.

"Dare I?" Anne asked, adding a quick "why not?"

Violating the dress code she'd adopted during her Ivy League M.B.A. training, she freed her hair, fluffed it about her shoulders, and ruffled her bangs. Grinning defiantly, she topped her hair with the bright headband.

She turned and posed for Bella. "So much for sensibility today. Who cares anyway? A bunch of Wall Street-types fixated on debits-credits? I think not."

She had yet to meet the acquisition team--she'd only heard that some Eastern big boys were arriving with a ream of papers that would authorize the transfer of another company's name to the letterhead of Livingston Enterprises' stationery. A few strokes of a pen and it would be a done deal. Finis. Roll tape.

Anne shuddered. The finality of her situation weighed heavily on her heart. She thought about her employees and then about herself. Although thankful she'd been able to negotiate equitable separation compensation for most of her staff, she worried about her decision to request none for herself. My pigheaded Livingston pride, she thought. C'est la vie.

"There's no turning back now so I might as well get it over with. I'll be home early," she called to Bella as she headed for the front door.

She'd dreaded this day for weeks, but she knew she had to play her part with dignity. Taking a deep breath, she slowly opened the door and looked for a cab.

When one careened around the corner, she stepped to the sidewalk and waved. Noting the numbers painted on the taxi's fender, she said, "All zeros. It figures."

Bringing his cab to a squealing curbside stop, the driver asked, "Where to?"

"Livingston Centre on Government." She almost choked on the words.

"Too bad about that place. I hear it may be razed. Good spot for a casino, don't ya think?"

Unable to trust her voice, Anne studied a newspaper someone had left behind. The business page headline flashed at her--"The Livingston Centre Story: The Last Chapter."

Trembling, she picked up the paper but quickly turned it over. She didn't want to read about her meteoric rise to power and subsequent fall from grace.

The driver slowed his cab to a crawl as it approached a tower made of glass and granite. "This is it. Looks empty."

Anne took some money from her wallet. Handing it over the front seat to the cabbie, she waved off the change he offered in return.

"Thanks, ma'am," he said, "I appreciate the tip, but don't you think you're gonna need this cash?"

"What?" she asked as she gathered her belongings.

"Recognized you from a picture in today's paper. Aren't you Bull Livingston's granddaughter?"

Anne's stiffened body language answered for her.

"Thought so. Well, good luck, missy. Sounds like you're in for a rough time."

Anne watched the taxi spin off. "Damn," she swore quietly. "I hate everything about this day--pity from strangers, regrets from competitors, good-byes from colleagues...Saints above, give me strength to get through this."

"Good morning, Miss Livingston," the doorman said with a smile and a tip of his cap. For four years, he'd welcomed her this way.

Anne returned the man's smile but sadness clouded her eyes as she greeted him for the last time.

Walking on through the reception lobby, Anne felt a lump rise in her throat when she passed by a family photo taken a month before her grandfather had planned to retire and hand the company over to his only child, Anne's father.

Such a happy time, she recalled, when everyone had been so excited, especially Bull. Anne could still hear him say, his voice ringing with pride, "My boy's ready and I'm rarin' to trade in this ol' briefcase for a tackle box. Thirty days and I'm gone fishin'."

A telephone rang in an outer office reminding her of the call from the Coast Guard that had turned Bull's joy and anticipation to grief. A fatal boating accident in raging Gulf waters had claimed Bull's son, his daughter-in-law, and grandson.

Within days, Bull's plans had changed and so had Anne's life. Fresh out of graduate school, she'd found herself facing challenges she'd only studied in management casebooks. But determined to pull her own weight, she'd blossomed as she mastered one challenge after another.

With Bull as her mentor and a bit of luck, she'd restructured Livingston Enterprises into a Fortune 500 company. Those had been the halcyon days; today was a totally different story.

As she walked through the quiet halls of the executive suite, she missed hearing a busy hum, happy chatter. The silence felt odd, strange, deathly.

Before entering her office, she stopped to fix a cup of hot tea. She reached into the drawer where she stashed her favorite herbal blends. Expecting to find a packet of Red Zinger, she found instead a fresh box of honeyed chamomile with a note attached--"This'll calm the last day jitters, kitten. You're the best and I'm proud of you. Love ya, darlin', Bull."

A tear slipped from the corner of Anne's eye as she hurried to her desk. There she sat in Bull's mahogany and leather chair that dwarfed her petite figure. Unable to part with its familiar squeaks and squeals, she'd ignored numerous decorators' suggestions that she change it out for one more fitting her size. She wondered if the new owners would keep it around. Thinking, probably not, she turned to the work on her desk.

She thumbed through a stack of legal papers but stopped when she felt someone watching her. Thinking her secretary, Brittany, had come in, she didn't look up. Instead, she sipped her tea and said, "Short day ahead. Let's do it."

"Okay," sounded a deep voice.

Anne caught her breath when she looked up. Her eyes locked with those of one of the handsomest men she'd ever seen. She gasped and felt her cheeks burn.

"Sorry, I didn't mean to startle you. No one was at the front desk. I saw your light, so I came on in."

Anne remained silent. He had to be one of them, one of the suits from New York, she surmised. After weighing the pros and cons of civility, she asked, "Are you lost or just anxious?"

"Excuse me?"

Anne checked her watch. She wasn't due in the boardroom for an hour.

"May I ask who you're looking for?" She figured he'd wandered into the office ahead of schedule, probably to check out the amenities before his colleagues had a chance to survey the spoils.

He smiled disarmingly. "I'm sorry. I should have explained..."

"Explained what?" Anne interrupted him, a bit more curtly than she'd intended.

"I'll start over. I'm Stephen Richards, here for a meeting with Ms. Anne Livingston. When do you expect her?"

"Pardon?"

"Ms. Livingston, your boss," he answered, nodding toward the large brass nameplate on the desk. "You must be her assistant, Brittany. Haven't we talked on the phone?"

Miffed, Anne narrowed her eyes. Although she'd been mistaken for office staff before, she was highly offended this time. Huh, she thought, surely this seemingly intelligent, good-looking man should be able to tell who I am--I think I'll teach him a lesson.

"Well, Mr. Richards," she drawled, "I imagine Miss Livingston is already in the boardroom. She doesn't waste time." Anne marveled that she'd emphasized "Miss" and had barely mumbled "Livingston."

"Yes, I've heard about 'Miss' Livingston's toughness."

Hearing "Miss," she smiled.

"Is she really as hard as nails?" he continued.

"Harder," Anne said, hastily adding a polite "sir."

"Well then," he said, "if you'll point me in the right direction, I'll go prepare myself."

"I probably should point you right down the elevator shaft," Anne whispered under her breath.

"Did you say something?"

"Take the first right after you pass the elevator and you'll be in the boardroom. If you'd like some coffee, a refreshment area's on the left."

"Thanks," he said, winking wickedly.

She looked down, not wanting him to catch her reaction. Peeping from underneath her thick lashes, she watched him walk away. He looked good, real good, tall, broad shouldered, a hunk with an attitude. But what did he think of her?, she wondered.

Reality check time, Anne, she chided herself. She hated that she'd allowed herself to blush like a lovesick virgin. But most of all, she regretted wearing the headband. Worrying that she appeared unprofessional, she started to take it off.

Then she changed her mind, saying, "Wait a minute. I'm still in control here." Adjusting her hair, she gave it an extra fluff for good measure, all the while thinking, who cares what Stephen Richards thinks?--his opinion really doesn't matter, he's nothing to me.

Still though, she couldn't shake the memory of his deep blue eyes smiling into hers. She could sense he'd liked what he'd seen. But she wondered why she cared.

Her musings stopped when Brittany bustled through the door.

"Sorry I'm late. Traffic was a mess. Did I miss something? You look excited."

"Oh, hi." Anne fought to control the color she felt rising in her cheeks. Restacking the papers in front of her, she explained, "It's just the pressure of today."

While Anne centered herself for the meeting, Stephen tried to do the same. But he couldn't. Thoughts of the woman he'd just met filled his head--all women should look so good in pinstripes, and she had the sweetest Southern accent he'd ever heard, one he wouldn't mind hearing again, soon.

He poured a second cup of coffee, reminding himself that he needed to focus on the business at hand. After all, he'd come to Mobile to consummate the Livingston deal, not to make time with the company's sexy secretary.

Sighing, he walked into the boardroom that was draped in heavy damask and lit by a huge crystal chandelier. Thinking the fixture had to have cost a mint, he calculated its replacement value and shook his head at the amount. Then he touched the smooth surface of the focal point of the room, a highly polished teak conference table the likes of which he'd only seen in movies.

A few minutes later, other men wearing dark suits and shiny shoes entered the room. Nodding to Stephen, they jockeyed for power positions around the table. Stephen noticed his five-man team congregated to one side, virtually forcing the Livingston people into a face-off situation. Them against us, he thought.

Although initially distracted by a heated exchange that had begun between two Livingston VPs, Stephen kept staring at the captain's chair at the head of the table that remained unoccupied.

Noting Stephen's seeming preoccupation with the chair, one of his colleagues, sneering slyly, commented, "For Ms. Livingston, I presume."

"Of course," Stephen replied. "What do you think she..."

Before he could finish his question, though, a woman wearing sensible oxfords and a dark dress bustled breathlessly into the room. She smiled apologetically toward Stephen and then handed a note to one of the Livingston men.

Glancing at the message, the VP nodded and said, "Thanks, Brittany. I'll take care of this now." Excusing himself, he followed her out the door, closing it firmly behind.

"Brittany?" Stephen asked, arching his dark eyebrows quizzically. The "Brittany" he'd just talked with had baby blue eyes, long brown hair, and wore a striped business suit. This "Brittany" had fashionably cropped grey hair, brown eyes, and freckles.

Stephen didn't have to toy very long with the concept of two "Brittanys" in the Livingston secretarial pool. His puzzling ceased when a petite woman wearing a bright red headband entered the room.

Conversation stopped and all attention shifted to the woman whose eyes flashed blue fire in Stephen's direction. She smiled when she saw him catch his breath in surprise.

"Hello, gentlemen. Welcome to Livingston Enterprises. We have lots of work on the table, so let's get to it."

Outwardly she appeared cool and collected, but inside she felt a deep sadness as the emotions of the moment tugged at her heart. Not about to give away her true feelings, she calmed her spirit by reaching inside the pocket of her suit for the tiny sand dollar she carried as her lucky charm.

Without skipping a beat, she attended to the business of the day. Documents in triplicate changed hands, routine questions were posed and then answered, and before lunch, the transaction was finished.

Anne sat tall in her chair, studying the last document she'd signed. Livingston Enterprises was now history and Anne Livingston was unemployed.

CHAPTER 2

"Bella, Bella? Where are you?" Anne called softly. "I'm home. Please come here. I need to hold you."

Anne pitched her keys on the dresser and tossed her briefcase on the bed. Kneeling down, she peeked underneath her white eyelet bedskirt. There she found Bella, curled up on the floor and sleeping soundly.

"So this is how you spend your afternoons? Well, don't let me interrupt. No reason for you to change your routine just because mine's out of kilter, but I could use some company. Want to help with the mail?"

When Bella shifted her position and yawned broadly, Anne sighed, "Guess not."

She glanced through the envelopes and sorted out the advertising from the rest. "I really hate this," she said, worried that checking the mail and talking to her cat might become her only activities. "I've got to find another job, soon, tomorrow. But where?"

She changed out of her suit into jeans, a sweatshirt, and tennis shoes and curled up on her sofa. Picking up a Newsweek, she flipped through it, but put it aside ten minutes later. Bored, she realized she didn't know how to handle free time.

"Surely there's something I can do." She surveyed her living room. Nothing was out of place. She entered her kitchen and said, "That's it, the dishes. I'll rearrange them." She lugged a stool over to the counter, climbed up, and started stacking bowls next to salad plates and cups beside saucers. "Ah, that's better," she said, admiring her work.

Then she looked at her watch--only eight minutes had passed.

"That does it. I've got to get out of here," she announced to the kitchen sink. She ran a comb through her hair, grabbed her keys and some change, and headed to the front door. She paused on her porch, not sure which way to go. Then she heard the sound of small children playing and turned in the direction of the park just down the street.

At the playground, she watched some preschoolers taking turns on the swings and slides. She nodded to a young woman standing watchfully by who smiled sweetly and then turned away, her attention focused on the baby she nestled in her arms. Anne felt her heart ache.

She remembered when she'd dreamed about love, marriage, babies, and a big house fronting Mobile Bay. But that dream had fallen apart when she'd learned the love she believed in was false. She'd sworn never to give her heart away again. Instead, she'd pledged her loyalty to her work, something finite that would never let her down. At least, that's what she'd thought then.

"Daydreaming, Miss Livingston?"

Turning quickly, Anne caught her breath. Behind her stood Stephen Richards. The highlights of his dark hair shimmered gold and his eyes fairly danced. Anne couldn't help but stare.

"No, not really," she stammered. "But why are you here? Shouldn't you be off somewhere toasting your success with your pals?"

Stephen paused, stung by her comment. "A bar scene isn't my style. A walk in the park appeals lots more to me than a martini with a twist. I find joy in nature, makes me feel whole."

Anne rolled her eyes, thinking, oh brother, a poet's soul underneath a Ralph Lauren shirt and a fancy tie. She smiled.

"What's so funny? The trick you played on me this morning?"

"Miss Brittany?" she teased.

He nodded and grimaced beguilingly.

"Look, you made the mistake."

"True. It was just that..."

"What?" she asked.

"Let's say you caught me by surprise," he answered. He remembered how beautiful and sexy she'd looked. She still did. He wondered how she'd feel in his arms. Then, he reminded himself that he'd imposed a moratorium on relationships with women, at least with the dangerous type, those who could make a man fall in love and then break his heart. He already knew all about that.

Ignoring a voice inside his head that said, "Better watch out," Stephen took a closer look at Anne. She was something else, a woman who looked as desirable in sweats as she did dressed to the nines. Then he visualized her undressed-- his physical reaction made him catch his breath. So much for logic and caution, he thought.

What Stephen didn't realize was that he wasn't the only person dueling with an internal alarm system. At that very moment, Anne's was shooting off flares labeled "Be careful" and sparks named "You don't really know this man." Even so, she could feel her head spin and her heart soften.

Their attraction was shared, but unacknowledged.

At the corner of Church Street, Anne instinctively turned in the direction of her home. She listened to Stephen's talk of mergers and pay-outs, all the while wondering if he had a particular destination in mind or if he planned to follow her to her door. She considered interrupting him to ask, but didn't. She liked the sound of his voice too much.

"I'm sorry," he apologized. "Business talk is probably not what you want to hear."

"Oh, I don't know. Corporate deals have been my life for the last few years. I wonder if I can survive outside of that cocoon."

Feeling her vulnerability, Stephen wanted to fold her tightly in his arms. He knew she'd been through hell that morning and had to be hurting still. He wanted to comfort her, but he feared coming on to her too fast too soon. He thought he'd better try words instead of actions.

"Come on now, Miss Livingston. You're strong, a survivor. I saw that today. You handled a tough situation better than anyone I've ever seen."

Appreciating his words, Anne heard herself say, "Why don't you drop the 'Miss Livingston' and call me 'Anne'?"

Oh, Anne, he thought, how I'd like to drop all formality and whisper indecent sweetnesses into your cute little ears, all night long. He smiled lustily.

Hurriedly, Anne explained, "I meant nothing improper. It's just that now that I'm an ex-CEO I think I'd better get used to being just plain 'Anne.'"

He knew "just plain Anne" she'd never be.

"You're smiling again. Why?"

"Trust me, Anne. There's nothing plain about you," he answered, gazing into her eyes. "And please, call me 'Stephen.'"

"Deal." She noticed he'd slowed his pace to match hers or was she increasing hers to equal his?

They walked toward a small cafe. Stephen noticed Anne hesitate.

"Are you hungry?"

Realizing all she'd had that day was a cup of tea, she answered, "Starving."

"Me, too," he said, thinking that he'd become suddenly ravenous in more ways than one. "Let's go in."

Sounds of soulful jazz welcomed them inside. Ignoring the set of large booths that lined one wall, Stephen led Anne to a small table set for two. He wanted to sit as close to her as possible.

"This is nice," he said, looking around the room. Large Boston ferns and oak ceiling fans softened the simple decor. "Smells good, too," he added. "Is this what's called the 'intoxicating aroma of the leisurely South'?"

Anne laughed. "Are you making fun of my hometown?"

"Not a chance," he answered, smiling into her eyes.

He studied her delicate features--pretty eyes, upturned nose, inviting mouth. Oh, how he liked to look at her. So pretty, he thought, enjoying the way her heart-shaped face lit up and her blue eyes sparkled when she smiled. He liked her smile best of all.

"Ahem. Ready to order?"

"Oh, hi," Anne said as she picked up a menu and studied it briefly.

Stephen looked inquisitively at the burly waiter.

Eyeballing Stephen closely, the man said gruffly, "I'm Max. This is my place and I know Anne. What d'ya want?"

Winking at Max, Anne ordered two cups of cafe au lait.

Max frowned. "You sure? Most Yankees don't like chicory."

"I'm game," Stephen said.

"I'll bet you are," Max muttered as he stalked toward the kitchen.

"What gives?" Stephen asked.

Anne explained that Max had watched her grow up in the neighborhood and had taken a fatherly interest in her when she'd lost her family.

Stephen's heart went out to Anne when she told him about her personal tragedy. Only brief mention of the accident had been made in the background material he'd read in preparation for the Livingston assignment.

"No wonder Max is so protective."

"He's been a good friend."

Still scowling, Max trundled out with two cups of cafe au lait and a plate of beignets. "Still like these?" he asked Anne.

"What are they?" Stephen asked.

"A present for my favorite customer--a lady I care about," Max replied, emphasizing "lady." Casting a stern look toward Stephen, he added, "She's special around here, mister."

"I can see that." Stephen didn't need convincing. He'd already decided Anne was very precious and becoming more so with each moment they shared.

"What do you think?" Anne asked, watching Stephen's lips pucker at his first taste of strong coffee.

"Not bad," he said, "but I think I'll like the beignets better."

"Me, too," she said, selecting a puffy one. When she took a bite, confectioners sugar flew everywhere.

"Here, allow me." Stephen reached across the table to brush away the specks of flaky sugar that trailed from Anne's lips to her dimpled chin. The softness of her skin and the wetness of her lips made him almost forget where he was. Feeling very warm, he loosened his tie and undid the top button of his shirt.

When Anne noticed curly hairs emerge from his opened collar, she felt a surge of heat race through her as an image popped in her mind. "My, my," she gasped, embarrassed she'd just pictured where she'd find more of those same dark curls on Stephen's body.

Knowing she'd turned crimson, she said, "There's nothing like the warming effect of hot coffee."

Stephen was charmed by the rosy hue of Anne's cheeks. He couldn't remember the last time he'd seen a woman blush. He hoped it was he and not the coffee that had caused her reaction. As for how she affected him, the answer to that would've been no secret had he stood up.

Leaning forward, he reached for her hand. Their fingers touched and their eyes flashed golden as something new, something exciting, passed between them.

Neither spoke. They weren't given a chance.

A well-dressed man in his early thirties pushed his way inside the cafe, shouting, "Hot damn! Can it be Anne Livingston?"

"Oh, my goodness! Taylor! I haven't seen you since the SAE formal years ago."

"Give this man a kiss if you're glad to see him."

Anne pecked him on the cheek and said, "Please join us." Turning to Stephen, she explained, "This is Taylor Hamilton. We were classmates at the University in Tuscaloosa. Taylor, I'd like for you to meet Stephen Richards, he's here on business."

"That isn't what it looked like from outside," Taylor said shaking a finger naughtily at Anne. Then he pulled up a chair and started talking. "Yeah, we go way back. You remember tail-gatin' before the games?"

Anne nodded.

"The road trip to Mardi Gras?"

"Yes, Taylor. How could I forget when we had to make bail for you?"

"Right, heh heh. What about spring break at the Gulf?"

"That was another adventure."

"And another time," Stephen muttered. He felt his blood run cold. He wanted to throw this character out of Anne's life, but he knew he had no right. They obviously shared a history and he was the odd-man-out. His body tensed at the thought.

Sensing Stephen's mood swing, Anne tried to draw him into the conversation. "Did you know that you and Taylor both work in high finance?"

"Yeah, I just love makin' money. What about you, Steve, ol' boy?"

Stephen wanted to vaporize Taylor, not answer him. He disliked everything about the man, his Armani suit, sun-bleached hair, grinning face, and most of all, his obvious attraction to Anne.

He clenched his teeth when Taylor placed his arm behind Anne's chair. And when Taylor moved his hand to her shoulder, Stephen tightened his fist. Unable to stand another moment, he said, "Sorry to break this up, but I'm booked on a morning flight to D.C." Then he deftly moved to assist Anne with her chair. He'd hoped to spend the rest of the evening with her, but Taylor seemed to have the same plan.

"Cab service runs pretty good around here. Phone's out there, boy." Taylor motioned toward the street.

"Taylor! Be nice," Anne fussed.

Stephen bristled and said, "I'm seeing Anne home and we'll see you later."

"Hell no, I just got here." Taylor narrowed his eyes at Stephen as though he planned to break him in half. "Besides, didn't you say you have a plane to catch?"

"In the morning," Stephen answered curtly. He tossed several dollar bills on the table and reached for Anne's hand. Leading her to the door, he protectively placed his hand at the small of her back.

"Damn Yankee," Taylor cursed. "Wait up, I'm comin', too."

Max shook his head as he watched the threesome head down the street with Anne pinned between two large, fuming men. Pocketing the money Stephen had left behind, he grumbled, "Anne's had troubles enough. What now?"

Anne, Stephen, and Taylor walked in silence. When they reached Savannah Street, Anne broke the quiet by saying, "I see my house."

"You still live in the same place?" Taylor asked.

Stephen didn't like the tone of familiarity he heard in Taylor's voice. It sounded as though he'd been at Anne's before, maybe often.

"And that same old cat?" Taylor added.

"Well, you know me," Anne answered. "When I find something I like, I stick with it."

Listening to her every word, Stephen wished Anne would decide she liked him. The thought of her body stuck to his made his heart pound.

"You haven't changed much, Miss Annie," Taylor replied, thinking it was too bad she hadn't filled out more. He liked his women big, buxom, and bad. "Bet you still carry that loyalty bit of yours to extremes."

"What's he talking about?" Stephen asked.

Stiffening, Anne answered sharply, "A dead, boring issue." She knew Taylor was referring to the time she'd remained true to her fiance who'd betrayed her and laughed as he'd strolled out the door with one of her Phi Mu sorority sisters.

Sensitive to Anne's body language, Stephen quickly changed the subject. "What's the best way back to my hotel?"

Anne beamed her gratitude to him. Although he'd represented the opposition during her acquisition ordeal, he seemed like a nice person, a man she'd like to know better. She wondered what would happen if he stayed in town. Thinking she'd never find out, she turned her attention to Taylor. Seeing him briefly was one thing, spending time with him was something else.

"I have an idea, Taylor."

"What?"

"Is your car close by? How about taking Stephen to his hotel?"

"Yes, Taylor, ol' boy, how about a ride?" Stephen wanted to keep Taylor as far away from Anne as possible.

Liking the idea of having Anne indebted to him, Taylor rubbed his chin and said, "Anything to make the lady happy. I'll bring my car around."

Stephen breathed a sigh of relief. "Finally a moment's peace."

"I know. He talks a lot." She thought about Taylor's insensitivity and Stephen's thoughtfulness and wished Taylor had the morning flight to catch, not Stephen. A frown creased her brow as she tried to reconcile her feelings for Stephen. Nothing made sense. Although she'd just met him and under the worst of circumstances, she didn't want him to leave Mobile.

"Is something wrong?" he asked gently, not wanting to pry.

"This has been a tough day. It's hard for me to let go of things I care about."

"I know how you feel," he answered. Parting from Anne was more difficult than he'd anticipated. He wondered how he, the cautious no-commitment king, had become so deeply attracted to a woman he'd met only hours earlier. Maybe he did need the rest his coworkers had urged him to take. Some time off might help him get his head straight.

"How hot does it get in Alabama this time of year?" he asked.

"Excuse me?"

"Never mind." He decided the temperature wasn't important--a good thawing out might be exactly what he needed. And maybe Anne Livingston was the one to do it.

A sleek, burgundy Lexus rounded the corner and skidded to a stop. Taylor lowered a window and huffed at Stephen, "Get in." He winked at Anne and said, "You owe me, Annie doll."

Stephen started to say something to Anne, but Taylor revved the engine and leaned long and hard on the horn.

Anne watched the car pull away and started walking toward her townhome. She suddenly felt cold and very much alone.

As Taylor drove, Taylor bragged, mainly about his high roller deals and high dollar women. Stephen soon tuned him out. Redrawing Anne's features in his mind's eye was much more to his liking.

He pictured her long brown hair, her smiling eyes, and her sensual lips. Then he thought about her soft, creamy skin and the heat of her fingertips.

"Are you listening?" Taylor asked, clearly irritated.

"Sure." During the rest of the drive, Stephen humored him with a few "ohs" and "I sees." Anything Taylor said was okay by Stephen as long as Anne didn't figure in the jerk's plans.

While Taylor rambled, Stephen gave his imagination free rein. He mentally discarded Anne's clothing, one piece at a time. He imagined caressing her, loving her. Oh yes, he thought. He knew he had to talk to her again.

Thinking, tonight, I'll talk to her tonight. But about what? My feelings? No way, not yet. Wait, I've got it! I must apologize. What was I thinking to let her walk back to her home alone? I'll call her.

Taylor stopped the car. Stephen didn't notice. Thoughts of Anne had consumed his mind--how she'd fluffed her hair against the silk blouse she'd worn at the office. He shuddered as he got out of Taylor's car.

"Catch a chill?" Taylor asked.

"Nope, got a fever," Stephen answered with a knowing smile. And he knew where to find the cure. In a townhome on Savannah Street in downtown Mobile, Alabama.

"What a day," Anne said to Bella, now wide awake and hungry. "I've never felt so turned around. Oh, Bella, I'm confused. I know I should feel awful about my company, but all I can think about is Stephen, Stephen Richards."

Anne walked to the refrigerator. Bella followed close behind, purring in anticipation. Anne chose Dairy Cat for Bella and spinach for herself. Although she wasn't hungry, she fixed a light salad as Bella lapped up her milky treat.

After dinner, Anne settled down with a book she'd been meaning to read. Feeling guilty, she closed it and reached

for her personnel folder instead. She knew she should up-
date her resume since she planned to start her job search
the next day.

Somehow, though, she wasn't ready for today to end.
"How weird," she said aloud. "This morning all I wanted was
for today to be over--fast."

Bella jumped into Anne's lap, knocking the resume to
the floor.

"Oh, Bella. How am I ever going to get any work done?"
she scolded half-heartedly. Anne's thoughts were so scat-
tered that she didn't really mind the distraction. One second
she thought about a new job, the next instant she craved
a chocolate sundae, but most of all she wondered if she
could will her telephone to ring.

After staring at the phone for ten minutes, she tossed her
hands in the air in disgust. "Who am I kidding, Bella? I'm
twenty-eight, old enough to know better. Who's going to
call? Taylor Hamilton? Probably not. Stephen Richards?
Not a chance."

But oh, how she wanted that phone to ring.

Anne was wrong thinking she was on no one's mind. In
fact, across town in two different places were two men whose
only bond was their interest in the same woman. Neither
could shake Anne's image from his mind.

Taylor poured a double shot of whiskey before checking
in with his home base in Atlanta.

"Perfect day. Piece of cake...smooth as glass. The acquisition boys are clueless...they don't know who they really
represented...unbelievable but true. I even spent some time
with one, a typical Eastern dumb butt."

Taylor laughed so loudly he had to put the phone down.
He left the line open while he fixed another drink.

"I'm back. Listen to this...the one who got Anne's signature is sweet on her. She should hate his guts, but I think
he's softened her up. Hell, doesn't matter, I'll make sure
she changes her mind...but that's not real important--what
matters is that Livingston Enterprises now belongs to a
mystery man, me."

He chortled louder than ever and then hung up without saying "good-bye."

He thought about Anne. Pretty, trusting, honorable...an easy mark. Sweet, unsuspecting Anne, he mused, she must have missed the lesson on takeovers and dogs in mangers. Oh well, she'll be all right, he reasoned, especially if she marries her company's new owner. "Hot damn," he chuckled as he thought about bedding her. Stealing her company wasn't enough, he decided he might as well take her body, too.

Excited, he smacked his lips. He could taste her. He picked up the phone to call her, but decided to wait. He had a better plan. For now he'd keep an eye on her and make his move later.

Smiling devilishly, he turned his attention to other matters on his Rolodex.

Stephen studied his reflection in the mirror. He wondered what Anne saw when she looked at him. Could she tell he worked out regularly? Took care of himself? Did she like his body? He hoped so because he coveted hers.

"Hmm," he mused, thinking about Anne, relationships, the risks, the rewards. "Dare I try again?" he asked as he turned away.

He remembered the excitement he'd felt one time before when he thought he'd found his true love and was ready to commit. Before proposing, though, he'd learned it wasn't Stephen Richards his intended wanted--she was after all he represented. That's when he decided business was a safer mistress than love. If a deal didn't work, he could walk away and start over. But when hearts broke, the shattered pieces were harder to put back together.

Few people understood his feelings, somehow he bet Anne would.

Wanting to talk to her, he thumbed through the "Livingston" business cards he'd collected. He found those for the two men who'd sat across from him at the conference table. Bruce Floyd, V.P. for Finance, and Michael Adams, Professional Relations V.P. Discarding those, he compulsively searched for Anne's.

"Where is it? I know I didn't lose it. Anne Livingston, where are you?" he shouted aloud.

Remembering that she'd pointed to her townhome at the end of Savannah Street, he grabbed the phone book. Finding the "L's" and then the "Li's," he scanned the list until he found "Livingston: Abigail, AC, AE, AL, Alice, Alvin, Amelia."

"But where's Anne? And why aren't the addresses listed?" he fumed.

Frustrated, he decided to call every Livingston in the book until he found Anne. He knew he wouldn't rest until he heard her honeyed voice one more time.

"Sorry, wrong number."

Silent hang-up.

No answer.

"Get a life, buster."

Then he heard a soft, sugar-sweet "Hello?" He'd dialed the right number.

"Hello, Anne. I guess you don't know who this is," he stammered. He hated that he sounded like a backward clod instead of a confident, thirty-two-year-old man.

"No, I'm sorry I don't," she answered although she thought she recognized the deep voice.

"This is Stephen, Stephen Richards."

She held her breath.

"There's something else we should take care of before I return to my office in Providence."

When she didn't answer, he fumbled for a plausible reason he thought she'd accept. "I need your signature on another transfer sheet."

"Oh, I see." Disappointed, she sank into her chair, thinking, business, purely business.

"So, tomorrow..."

"Tomorrow? But...your flight to D.C.?" she asked, feeling a catch in her throat.

"Change of plans. So...would you like to do lunch? You name the place, somewhere special."

"Okay. How about the Port O' Call on the Eastern Shore at noon?"

"It's a date," he answered.

"But you don't have a car?"

"I'll rent one. Business expense--you know how that goes."

"Used to," she mumbled.

"You will again," he reassured her.

"I hope so," she said with a sigh. After giving him directions to Fairhope, she rang off with a "See you tomorrow."

She turned down her bed, upset she hadn't offered to pick him up at his hotel. Then she reasoned that might seem unprofessional, especially since he'd clearly indicated their meeting was for business. Oh well, it's probably better this way, she thought. But a part of her still wished they'd made plans for a real date.

Anne crawled under the covers and closed her eyes. Falling asleep, she dreamed about Stephen, reliving the moment their fingertips had touched.

* * * * *

Slipping into bed, Stephen thought of Anne. He wanted her beside him but not there. A hotel room was out of the question--she deserved a palace. Then, he chided himself for not owning up to why he'd really called her. Business wasn't what he wanted, she was.

CHAPTER 3

A new day and everything looked different. The more Anne thought about Livingston Enterprises, the angrier she became. Her life had been turned upside down and she was ready to assign accountability for the act. Someone would feel her fury.

"Why did I agree to meet that man for lunch? For God's sake, he helped terminate my career," she raged as she stalked around her bedroom. "I should've had him fax his idiot papers to me."

Then she remembered she no longer had a fax machine, hers was now out of order, permanently. "Acquired by the people who sign his paycheck," she fumed.

That did it, she made up her mind. She would simply ignore his rich dark hair, deep blue eyes, and boyish smile and see instead the man who worked for "them," the opposition. If Stephen Richards thought she was going to accept his last transfer documents gracefully, then he was in for the shock of his life. Yesterday she'd felt confused, stressed-out. Today she was just plain mad. Brimming with anger, she decided to show him firsthand what the term "Steel Magnolia" meant.

Pacing impatiently, Stephen studied a local map displayed in the hotel lobby. A trip across Mobile Bay to the Eastern Shore looked easy enough, tame compared to most other places.

"Mr. Richards?" The concierge smiled at Stephen and motioned for him to come to his desk.

"Yes?"

"Your car's around front. Here are the keys, rental agreement, and a message that just came in. Enjoy."

"Thanks," Stephen replied. He read the note quickly. His colleagues had arrived safely in Washington and were set for their next round of meetings. He was glad he'd sent them on ahead.

Free from work for a few days, he felt like a kid let out of school for summer vacation. He was ready to kick back and enjoy his time on the Gulf Coast. Especially having lunch with Anne.

"Let the good times roll," he sang as he popped open the car's sun roof, started the engine, and headed toward the Jubilee Parkway. He was glad the concierge had told him to allow extra time because the view of Mobile Bay was spectacular. Sailboats, coastal birds, blue skies, perfection.

Continuing along Highway 98, he slowed down to take in the sights. This is all right, he thought, as he entered Fairhope, a small village nestled high on a bluff overlooking the Bay. Thinking he had to have been transported to a Cape Cod village by mistake, he was quite taken with the place.

He backed his car into a parking space in front of a small apothecary and did a double take. Not only were there no parking meters in sight, there was no pollution in the air or litter on the streets. No wonder Anne likes this place, he thought as he left his car, without bothering to lock up.

Savoring the brisk sea air and the sun's soft rays, he envied the freedom of the bicyclists and joggers he watched on the paths beside the waterfront. Walking toward the center of town, he admired the bright flowers, big oaks, and quaint shops that lined the streets. This town's like Anne, he thought, beautiful, vibrant, hypnotic.

He heard bells from a tower sound eleven rings. Since Anne wasn't due for an hour, he decided to scout out the restaurant she'd selected.

So this is the Port O' Call, he mused. Before going in, he read the menu posted out front. Good choice, Anne, he thought--he was hungry for fresh seafood from the Gulf.

When he opened the restaurant's heavy cypress door, the aroma of crab boil awakened his senses. He made his way through the noisy crowd and exchanged friendly nods with some of the patrons. He moved to the only empty stool at the bar and positioned himself toward the front window so he could better watch for Anne.

"Can I get you something?" a waiter asked.

"Yeah. A draft and some oysters on the half-shell."

"Six of our finest headed your way, sir."

"Bring them on," Stephen said, settling in for an enjoyable afternoon. He glanced at some of the other men seated close by, noting that most were dressed like him, casual.

He was glad that he hadn't worn his dark suit because it would've stood out in contrast to the relaxed, yet moneyed, attire he saw around him. Hoping for some down-time, he'd brought along a pair of khaki pants and a navy blazer, just in case.

"Can I get you something else?" the waiter asked, placing Stephen's order in front of him.

"Tabasco sauce?"

"Yes, sir," he answered. "Guess you like 'em hot?"

Stephen smiled and said, "Sure do."

He thought about Anne and hoped she'd made it through the morning all right. He knew her first day away from her office had to be a shocker. Thinking of ways to get her mind off of her problems, he smiled. There were lots of pleasure paths he'd like to explore with Anne.

"This stuff'll burn you," the waiter warned as he handed Stephen a bottle of hot sauce. "Let me know when you need another beer."

"Sure....." Stephen was about to say more, but he was distracted by some women about Anne's age seated at a table by the window. He noticed that they wore gold necklaces of varying lengths and thought, Cartier, probably. Although the threesome made an attractive picture in their cotton sweaters, silk blouses, and patterned skirts, it wasn't their looks that caught his eye, but the name "Taylor Hamilton" on their lips that got his attention. Stephen shifted his weight toward the right so he could better hear their conversation.

A woman with light blond hair and heavy makeup giggled and said, "I heard Taylor was cruising Spring Hill the other night. Wonder what brought him back?"

A brunette with freckles commented, "Can't imagine. I heard he was Mr. Big in Atlanta. Worth millions now."

"How do you know?" the blond asked.

"A reliable source. My brother-in-law in Montrose handled some of Taylor's legal work so he ought to know."

"Just think...all that money and good looks, too. Maybe he's here for a vacation," the blond suggested.

A younger woman with jet black hair joined in, "No way. Taylor Hamilton doesn't rest. He's too busy making deals."

"A woman's involved," the brunette said, nodding her head for emphasis.

The blond agreed. "Yeah, a beautiful one with money, connections, or a business he wants. Taylor only travels with a purpose."

Stephen felt the pit of his stomach harden. Hearing Taylor Hamilton's name made him sick enough, but the thought of Taylor pursuing a beautiful woman, like Anne, especially Anne, made him lose his appetite.

He remembered how casually Taylor had slipped his arm around Anne the night before. Suddenly a wave of nausea passed through him. He wondered why he felt so strange? So clammy? Was it the food? The drink? The thought of Taylor pawing Anne?

He felt the room sway. Clenching his fists and closing his eyes tightly, he tried to rid his mind of thoughts of Taylor with Anne. But the offensive image wouldn't go away. Cursing Taylor, the oysters, and the beer, he felt the floor swallow him whole.

* * * * *

"Good," Anne said, finding a parking space across the street from the Port O' Call. She checked the time and seeing she was early, she walked into the Page & Palette, a bookstore that was sandwiched between a dress salon and a florist shop.

"May I help you?" a middle-aged clerk wearing horn-rimmed glasses asked.

27

"No thanks, I'm just browsing." To herself, she muttered, "I haven't a clue what I want."

"Did you say something about a clue? Do you like mysteries? What about a romantic mystery? Would you like that?" the clerk asked, trying to be helpful.

Anne thought for a moment and then answered, "Maybe that's just what I need--intrigue with a splash of romance."

Her mind momentarily flashed a scene of her and Stephen sharing kisses, quiet moments, and more. But she dismissed her thoughts as ridiculous.

"Our best sellers are over there," the clerk said. He nodded toward the front window.

Scanning the titles of a row of books placed at eye level, Anne felt as though someone outside was watching her. She peered around cautiously, but seeing no one, she turned her attention back to the books. She selected one and took it to the register.

"Excellent choice, a page-turner," the clerk said, smiling as he rang up the sale. "The story takes place in Memphis."

"Oh," Anne said, hoping he wouldn't spoil the ending.

"In a courtroom," he continued, but then he stopped and walked to the front of his store. "Look over there at the Port O' Call. Wonder what's the commotion?"

Anne picked up her book and raced across the street. The tower bells pealed out twelve rings as she reached the front door of the restaurant. Patrons lined the sidewalk in front, grousing about having to make room for some tall man who'd taken a dive from a barstool.

Inside, Anne found Stephen, ashen and shaky, seated at a table by the window.

"Here, pal," a waiter said, "drink this." He handed Stephen a glass of water.

Anne pushed her way through the crowd. She couldn't believe her eyes. Stephen looked as though he'd been steamrolled.

"Stephen? What happened?" She rushed to the table where he sat holding his head in his hands. She decided against laying him low and wondered who'd gotten to him first. She felt sorry for him and thought he needed a friend a lot more than a scolding.

But just as quickly as the Gulf weather changes, so did Anne's mood. Her thoughts of mercy switched to those of mayhem when she saw Marcie MacDonald, a former rival, playing cardiac nurse.

Disoriented, Stephen said, "Oh, Anne, I honestly don't know what happened. I was sitting over there, everything was fine, but then the room started spinning and I held on to keep from falling. After that, I don't know."

"Interesting," Anne murmured. Suspicion flickered in her eyes. "Tell me more."

"When I came to, I was sitting here."

Frowning, Anne asked, "What about her?"

"Her?"

"Her," Anne said, nodding toward the blond who'd placed her hand on Stephen's chest. Anne locked eyes with Stephen and said, "She has a name--Marcie."

"You know each other?" he asked, looking at the blond who batted her mascara-laden lashes and smiled icily.

"From way back when," she answered. "Good to see you again, Annie. You know this big fellow?"

"Yes, and I also know something about anatomy. If you're serious about finding his heart, your hand's in the wrong place."

Marcie giggled and stopped rubbing Stephen's left nipple. To Anne, she said, "You always were the smart one." To her girlfriends, she sniped, "I was the pretty one."

Furious, Anne retorted, "By the way, 'that big fellow' is my date." Her eyes flashed daggers at Marcie as she added, "He and I have lots to discuss, in private."

"Too bad for me," Marcie fumed. "It's not every day that a handsome guy falls at my feet."

"Sorry," Stephen apologized. "I hope I didn't crush you."

Ignoring Anne's glare, Marcie whimpered, "I didn't know that bruises could hurt so bad." Pouting, she pointed daintily toward her right hand and held it to Stephen's lips.

He knew he risked enraging Anne, but he felt responsible for Marcie's pain. After kissing her hand quickly, he apologized again, "I'm sorry I hurt you."

"Ooh, I feel so much better now." Marcie arched her chest toward Stephen and looked soulfully into his eyes. "If you ever need someone to soften your landing, let me know." Blowing him a kiss, she added, "I'm certified in CPR."

Looking to Anne for sympathy and finding none, Stephen shook his head and said, "This wasn't my fault. I don't know what happened."

A man wearing a grease-stained apron shouted from the kitchen, "Don't sue me. The oysters were fresh. I shucked 'em this mornin' myself so I know it wasn't 'em that got ya."

"I wish I had the answer, but I don't." Stephen shrugged his shoulders and then added softly, "I'm glad you're here."

He looked so miserable that Anne relented, saying "Oh, Stephen." The "Steel Magnolia" felt herself melt into a pussycat.

Looking directly into her eyes, he asked, "Can we start this afternoon over? Without Marcie, without oysters."

"Okay," she said, thinking that no harm could come from a routine business lunch.

But Stephen's thoughts were on anything but business. "This is the way I'd planned to greet you," he said, putting his arm around her shoulder and pecking her on the cheek.

"What are you doing?" she asked.

He smiled into her eyes. "I knew you were good medicine. Being with you makes me feel stronger."

"How strong?"

Lowering his arm to her waist, he said, "Strong enough to begin our date."

"Date?" She looked at him quizzically.

"Isn't that what you told Marcie?" Instantly, Stephen regretted mentioning the woman's name.

"Let's not talk about her." Anne flushed, causing her complexion to match the peach cashmere sweater she wore.

"And let's not sit here. It's more private over there." Stephen nodded toward an overstuffed booth anchored in a dimly lit corner. When he saw sparkles return to Anne's eyes, he took her hand, kissed it, and said, "Follow me."

She did.

And Stephen was thankful. Anne's beauty and style overwhelmed him. The way she looked, walked, and talked drove him to distraction.

He cleared the way for her through the crowded tables. Turning back, he watched her move gracefully behind him. He smiled as his eyes followed the gentle sway of her small hips.

At the booth, he stood back so Anne could pass in front of him. "Excuse me," he apologized, when his hand accidentally brushed against the fine fabric of her white skirt. Damn, he thought, how could such sweetness and fire inhabit one perfect body.

"What are you thinking?" she asked.

He reached across the table for her hand. "I think you know."

"What?"

"That you're beautiful," he answered, gently stroking her fingers.

She felt her cheeks warm with pleasure at his touch. Embarrassed, she decided to shift their talk away from her. "Good thing you got your strength back. Otherwise, Marcie might've compromised your virtue."

"Oh?"

"It's like this. If you want to fall on Marcie, you'll have to take a number." She waited for Stephen to react. His silence prompted her to add, "I should've asked how she and what's his name are getting along."

"Jealous?" he asked.

Anne huffed her reply, "I'm giving you insider information. I thought you'd appreciate the tip."

"She's not my type," he answered, smiling as he reached for a menu.

"See something you want?" she asked, her eyes wide with innocence.

He knew what he wanted, but he didn't say. Instead he watched Anne, loving her with his eyes.

Anne could feel her heart pull toward Stephen. Worrying that her mind might follow, she made herself bring up the subject of their business matters. "Aren't we here to finish our paperwork?"

"Yes."

"Well? Where are the papers?"

He reached into the breast pocket of his blazer.

As he did, Anne noticed his muscular chest. When he leaned forward, she thought about touching him, about how he'd respond. She thought she knew.

"Are you okay?" he asked, noticing Anne shiver slightly. Not waiting for her answer, he moved to her side of the booth and wrapped her securely in his arms. He liked the way she felt.

"Stephen!"

He released his hold and reached for his water glass. He thought he'd better cool it for now but he wasn't about to move back to the other side of the booth.

A smile teased the corners of Anne's lips. She liked the closeness of Stephen's body next to hers, especially his thigh rubbing against her leg and his arm brushing against hers.

"Now where were we?" Anne asked, trying to slow her heart rate that Stephen had caused to pick up a staccato beat. "Shouldn't we take care of business?"

"Okay, here goes." He unfolded a couple of pieces of paper. "I need your initials in the lower right hand corner."

Glancing at the document he placed in front of her, she asked, "Isn't this the retirement transfer authorization I signed yesterday?"

"Well yes, but..."

"But what?"

"See? It has two pages. I decided I should get your initials on the first one, as well as your signature on the second," he explained cagily.

Not fooled, she scribbled "AL" on the paper and gave it back to him. He quickly folded the document and returned it to his pocket.

"Is that all?" Anne asked.

"Yep."

"You stayed over just to have me initial a paper I'd okayed yesterday?"

"Yes and no."

She smiled as he fumbled for an explanation.

"Yes, I stayed an extra day in Mobile, and no, it wasn't just to have you initial a form."

"Go on."

But he didn't have to because a stately, older couple saved him.

"Anne, how lovely to see you on our side of the Bay," a woman wearing silk and pearls said warmly.

"But why are you in this dark corner? I don't think Bull would approve," the woman's companion said.

Stephen smiled at the couple, but they countered with curious stares.

"Mr. and Mrs. van Court, what a nice surprise. I'd like for you to meet Stephen Richards. He's in Mobile on business. I'm showing him another side of South Alabama."

"Oh? A business associate. How nice." Mrs. van Court replied.

Anne couldn't admit to these friends of her grandfather that she was socializing with a man who'd aided the end of Livingston Enterprises.

Smiling, Mrs. van Court continued, "I've been trying to reach you about a dinner we're having at Point Clear tomorrow night. We'd love for you to come. If you would like, please bring along your friend."

"Sure. That'll give me a chance to check him out for Bull," Mr. van Court added with a wink. "By the way, tell that ol' so and so I'd like to challenge him to a round of eighteen the next time I'm at Spring Hill,"

"He'd like that," Anne replied. "And thank you for the invitation, but Stephen has other plans. He..."

Stephen quickly interrupted Anne by saying, "Didn't I tell you that I'm staying here a while longer? So I'll look forward to your dinner, Mrs. van Court. Thank you for inviting me."

Mrs. van Court smiled and said, "Good. Anne, I'll call you with the details."

As the van Courts followed a waiter to their table, Anne looked at Stephen and bristled. "I can't believe you. What do you think they'll say when they find out why you came to Mobile?"

He shrugged his shoulders, ready to take a little heat from Anne. He remembered hearing that Taylor had been spotted at Spring Hill and he wanted to find out more about the man. Mingling with the inner social circle of the Eastern Shore might give him some answers.

Still fuming, Anne announced, "It's time to go."

"What about lunch?" Stephen asked, having recovered his appetite.

"I thought you were more interested in dinner plans," she said stormily.

Before he could answer, a waiter approached them holding a monogrammed, linen handkerchief. "I think this is yours, sir."

"Thanks. It must have slipped out of my pocket when I hit your deck," Stephen said, trying to make Anne laugh.

She wasn't amused.

"Let me walk you to your car," Stephen offered.

She didn't want to create a scene, so she said, "Suit yourself."

At her car, Stephen bent to open the door for her. But when he noticed where she'd parked, he said, "Wait here, I'll be right back."

"Where are you going?" she asked as Stephen moved out of sight. She didn't have long to wonder. He quickly returned carrying a ruby red rose in full bloom.

"What's this for?" Anne asked, surprised by the gesture.

"Peace offering?"

When Anne leaned toward the flower to sample its heady fragrance, a strong rush of wind surged by, scattering some petals.

"What the hell?" Stephen cursed as he watched a fast moving Lexus take a corner on two wheels and speed by. He thought he recognized the driver, but he didn't share his suspicions with Anne whose back was to the street. He didn't want anything to spoil his last minutes with her.

"I'll get you another rose."

"No way, I like this one's windblown look."

A breeze coming off the Bay ruffled Anne's hair. "Ah, that feels nice," she said, closing her eyes.

Stephen envied the wind that teased her long hair held loosely by a barrette. He wanted to undo its clasp so he could run his fingers through her waves that he knew would feel soft, silky. He imagined nestling his face into her hair and working his way down. But he knew he had to be patient.

He didn't want to frighten her with his blatant desire, but maintaining his composure was becoming almost impossible. He knew if she moved an inch closer to him, she would realize the power of her effect.

While he fought his sensations, she battled hers. There was no denying the attraction she felt for him. Demurely, she gazed into his eyes and gasped when she saw her hungry reflection looking back. Enticed by her need and his compelling maleness, she felt herself lean closer to him.

They almost touched, but the sound of bells reminded her it was mid-day on Section Street in downtown Fairhope. Stephen didn't care, but Anne did. When he reached for the curve of her spine, she gasped, "Oh my," and pulled away.

Reluctantly, Stephen opened her car door. Before closing it, he was tempted to trail kisses down her throat as she moved forward to adjust her seat belt.

Smiling sweetly into his eyes, she waved good-bye and put her car in gear.

Stephen watched her drive away. What a woman, he thought, she's special, maybe I'll tell her so at the dinner. Before then, though, he planned to run a trace on Taylor Hamilton. If Taylor posed any threat to Anne, Stephen wanted to be her savior.

Returning to his car, Stephen thought about the growing intensity of his feelings for Anne. She didn't have to be in the same room with him to arouse him. Just thinking of her caused his passion to spike.

He couldn't deny what had happened to him. He'd come to South Alabama on business to close a deal. That he'd accomplished but more had transpired. Stephen Richards had fallen in love.

CHAPTER 4

Anne threaded her car through the afternoon work traffic that trailed out of Mobile. Turning onto Government Street, she frowned, thinking, all these people have jobs and I just lost mine. "Unemployed" flashed through her mind. She shuddered and grasped her steering wheel tighter.

She remembered all the horror stories she'd heard about people reentering the job market. Not a good time to be out of work, she thought, doubting if she'd see an ad for a CEO in the afternoon Press Register.

Relocating was a possibility, but not a thought she relished. She hoped she wouldn't have to leave her grandfather and her home but she worried she might have no other choice. Upset and angry with herself for spending most of the day in Fairhope and not beginning her job search as she'd intended, she left her car at a parking garage and walked the short distance to her townhome.

Anne opened the door and almost tripped over Bella who was sound asleep on top of the mail that the postal carrier had dropped through the slot in the front door. With her cat in one arm and her mail in the other, she walked to her sofa and sat down.

"What's all this?" she said, as she sorted through the day's delivery of a magazine, an electric bill, a sweepstakes notice, and some advertising for personal products, namely condoms.

"I'll read this later," she said, quickly putting the magazine on her cherry coffee table. Peeking through the envelope of the electric bill, she shook her head and sighed, "This'll have to go in the secretary for now. I'll deal with my bills later, much later."

She tossed aside the contest entry and the condom ad, thinking both were a waste of her time. Maybe not, she thought, as she picked them back up and turned toward Bella. "If I won the $10 million cash prize, I'd buy the company back for me and boxcar loads of Sheba for you."

Bella snuggled closer to Anne and nibbled on the condom ad. "You want to see this?" she asked.

Anne took a closer look at the happy couple featured in the ad and thought about falling in love, having safe sex. She noticed how the man's hair was styled just like Stephen's, a bit long and kind of fluffy and so deeply dark that it was almost black.

Stop it, she thought, trying to stifle the images of Stephen that had taken up residence in her brain and in her heart. He was just passing time, held over in town without anything better to do--that's why he invited me to lunch, she reasoned.

Bella nuzzled Anne's arm as if to comfort her mistress.

"Anyway, Bella, he'd want someone equally successful, not me, a woman who's been removed from her office building as well as her desk."

She crumpled up the ads and said, "What's with me? I don't stand a prayer of either winning a million dollars or of falling passionately in love. It's not going to happen."

Changing out of her dress clothes, Anne reached for her sweats and socks. She neatly folded her sweater and put away her skirt and shoes. Turning away from her closet, she caught a glimpse of her reflection in the mirror. Wearing only lacy white panties and a matching bra, she stopped to look at herself.

Moving closer to the mirror, she started her visual self-exam from the top of her head down to her small bare feet. Bella, acting as though she didn't want to be left out, jumped up on top of Anne's dressing table and joined in the study of Anne Livingston. In unison, both leaned forward and then pulled back from the glass.

"Oh, geez," Anne said, "Look at my eyes. I need to get more rest. I bet Marcie never worries about wrinkles or dark circles." She exaggerated a smile, testing for fine lines, and shook her head sadly, saying, "Better call Avon, pronto."

Seeming puzzled by Anne's unusual activities, Bella cocked her head to one side and shifted her left ear forward.

"What do you see, Bella? Do you think my body's okay or do I need some liposuction here and a few tucks there?" Unable to see her own perfection, Anne grimaced as she pointed first to her firmly shaped thighs and then to her flat stomach, concluding, "A total makeover, that's what I need."

Bella yawned as if she'd lost interest and jumped down, flipping her tail high in the air as she sauntered away.

"Oh, well," Anne sighed. "It's too late for me. I'm a goner-- no job, no love life and not a sign of anything hopeful in my future."

Disgusted, she dressed quickly, slipped into her well-worn moccasins, and headed for the kitchen. Maybe a pot of tea will help, she thought, determined to shake her blues. Her intentions were golden, but her timing too late as she succumbed to a sudden attack of the "What ifs" before the water started to boil.

What if she'd done something differently to head off the takeover? What if she could somehow regain control of Livingston Enterprises? What if, what if?

She reached for a granola bar and her best china cup and saucer. Pouring her tea, she wished she could go back in time and relive some happy moments, like the ones she'd spent with Stephen. Then she recalled the role he'd played in her company's demise.

I don't get it, she thought, why am I attracted to him? I shouldn't feel anything but mistrust toward the man. For heaven's sake, he was there, putting the papers in my hand! She pursed her lips, swearing she would simply make herself forget how easily they'd talked, laughed, even flirted. She remembered how closely they'd sat together at the Port O' Call and how much she'd liked it. Oh brother, she thought, forgetting Stephen may take some work.

She curled into one of her wing chairs in the living room and motioned for Bella to hop up on her lap. In order to keep her left hand free to pet Bella's soft fur, Anne placed her tea on a small table on her right side.

Anne tried not to drop any crumbs from her snack, but a couple of falling bits of granola caused Bella to open one large eye. "Tell me, Bella, what is it about Stephen Richards that makes me feel so different? Why am I thinking about him now?"

Bella shifted slightly as if annoyed by Anne's chatter.

"Okay, I'll be quiet. Maybe I'll meditate a while."

She closed her eyelids and projected herself onto a sea-scape. Instead of picturing sea oats, sand, and a sunset, her mind placed her back at the Port O' Call with Stephen. She readied herself for action but before anything good could happen, she suddenly opened her eyes, thinking she'd heard her telephone ring. She leaned forward in her chair and listened intently, but then she fell back, disappointed.

Sorry, self, she thought, I can't help my feelings. I honestly wish he'd call. She wanted to hear the sound of his voice, his firmness when he made a point and his softness when he showed concern.

Lost in her thoughts, she jumped when the phone really did ring, once, twice, three times. "It's him, I know it's Stephen," she said, adding, "move, Bella, so I can get the phone." Bella suddenly felt like a forty pound sack of concrete on Anne's lap.

Thinking, relax, just calm down, she breathed deeply and said aloud, "If it's him, he probably only needs directions to the van Courts' party, that's all."

She cleared her throat and answered as normally as she could with a simple "Hello?"

"Stay with your own kind," said a voice sounding muffled and coarse.

"Excuse me?"

"You heard what I said," the voice growled and then the line went dead.

Anne sat for a few minutes holding the receiver in her hand. Stunned, she returned the handset to its base. She couldn't imagine who'd called or why. As for the person's gender, she didn't have a clue, the voice had sounded so garbled.

Then the phone rang again, causing chills to run down Anne's spine. First afraid to answer and then more frightened not to, she picked up the handset and shouted into the receiver, "This isn't funny."

"Anne, are you all right?" asked a definitely male voice.

Not recognizing the caller and with fear rising in her throat, she asked, "Who is this?"

"It's me, Taylor, Taylor Hamilton."

"Oh, Taylor," she said with a deep sigh of relief. "I'm glad it's you. I just had the strangest call."

"Really? What happened?"

"I'm not sure, but I think the caller threatened me."

"Threatened you? How?"

Anne trembled and answered, "I was warned to stay with my own kind. I don't get it, do you?"

"Look, I'll come over and we'll talk. You stay put and don't answer your door until I get there. Better let your answering machine screen your calls, you know, in case that devil tries again."

"Thanks, Taylor, but everything's really okay," she said, deciding she was overreacting. "It was probably a wrong number or a crank call. You don't need to rush over here."

"No problem, I'll be there in a flash," he answered firmly.

"There's really no need," Anne repeated, but Taylor had already disconnected and was on his way out the door.

Stephen pitched his blazer in a chair, kicked off his shoes, and flipped on the stereo in his hotel suite. Still feeling slightly queasy, he decided to rest a while before preparing for the evening. He reached for a brochure on his coffee table that listed local places of interest.

Turning to the section on the Eastern Shore, he scanned the description about Point Clear. Interesting, he thought, and then taking a closer look, he read aloud, "For about a century and a half, the Grand Hotel at Point Clear has hosted world dignitaries and the rich and famous." Thinking, this I've got to see, he continued reading, "a magnificent place of every creature comfort."

He sat back and let his mind conjure up all manner of romantic thoughts of wide verandas, sleeping rooms that opened onto arched, columned galleries, and soft Bay breezes. Just as he was ready to add some people to his scene, he noticed a yellow light flashing on the telephone in his bedroom.

"Wonder what's that about?" he said as he pushed the message retrieval number.

"This is Stephen Richards in Suite 904. Do I have a message?"

"Let me check," a clerk answered.

Stephen tapped his fingers on the nightstand, a fine 18th century reproduction.

"Sir?"

"Yes."

"Several messages were left for you today."

"Go ahead," he said, wondering if Anne had called. Then he considered that her upbringing probably precluded her from initiating such a call, so he dismissed the thought and reached for pen and paper to jot down his messages.

None of the calls seemed that pressing. His colleagues reported their meetings had been moved into the next week. Good, Stephen thought, they can do without me for a few days. I'm due some time away, he rationalized.

His secretary, Toni, had left word that a friend from Minneapolis was flying East for a skiing trip to Vermont and wanted to know if he'd like to join her. From the number she'd left, he knew the friend was a woman named Lisa. He started to write her number down but then scratched it out. He shook his head at the thought of champagne toasts and hot tubs with anyone except Anne.

He visualized warm, scented currents swirling around them. Tempted by the thought of aroma therapy and Anne's luscious body, he had to sit down.

"Sir? Are you still there?" the clerk asked.

"Yes, sorry. I got distracted," Stephen explained. "What did you say?"

"Someone left an envelope for you at the front desk."

"Oh really? Well, I'll pick it up on my way to dinner," Stephen said, ending the conversation.

An envelope? Wonder what it is?, he thought, knowing anything from the main office or the branches would've been faxed to the hotel. Curious, but wanting to shower and shave before beginning his evening, he stripped off his clothes, tied a towel around his waist, and turned on the water.

As he lathered his lean body with scented gel, he thought of Anne--the fragrance of her skin, the softness of her voice, her touch. He wanted to feel her long, silky hair wet and to see it glisten in starlight. Yes, he wanted her, but he wanted her to want him back.

After toweling off, he reached for a comb. Running it through his hair, he stared at his image in the foggy mirror and thought, how can I make Anne see that I'm not the villain in her company's takeover? Will she ever trust me? Really trust me?

He put on his shirt and reached for his khakis. After giving them a good wrinkle-removing shake, he pulled them on and reached for his belt. Buckling it around his waist, he patted his firm stomach and said aloud, "Better keep exercising, I don't want a gut like Taylor Hamilton's. Now there's one arrogant beast Anne should watch out for."

On his way downstairs, Stephen thought about Taylor and hoped Anne could see through Taylor's old ruse of pals from the past just happening to meet again. Stephen didn't believe Taylor for an instant, he prayed Anne didn't either.

At the front desk, Stephen studied the envelope with his name block printed across the front. Tearing into it, he stopped, surprised by the contents.

Oh, come on, this is junior high stuff, he thought. Not knowing whether to feel anger or humor, he examined a rough drawing of an oyster with a skull and crossbones etched beside it. Turning the sketch over, he read the words someone had printed sloppily on the back. "Leave ours alone, dig yours out of the Chesapeake Bay. Next time you won't be so lucky."

Stephen stormed back to the front desk and asked, "Do you know anything about this foolishness?"

"Something wrong, sir?" asked the clerk who'd handed Stephen the message.

"There certainly is. Were you on duty when this was left for me?" He shoved the ripped envelope under the clerk's nose.

"I've been here since noon, so I assume I was," the young man responded abruptly, seeming aggravated by Stephen's attitude. "Why?"

"Because I want to know what idiot left this trash for me."

The clerk stared blankly at Stephen and answered, "We have messenger deliveries in and out all day long. So there you go." Then he turned away.

"I see," Stephen seethed as he wadded the message into a ball and shoved it deeply into his pocket.

In a huff, he stalked into the coffeeshop and ordered a glass of Perrier with a lemon twist. He tried to work through all that had occurred that day, but nothing added up. Becoming suddenly ill was alien to his strong constitution. A man of robust health, he'd never been susceptible to sudden viruses and his stomach was pretty much cast-iron.

He decided there was only one logical explanation. "Someone did a 'Mickey Finn' number on my oysters and now they want me to know about it," he said, twisting his glass so hard that it slipped from his hand.

Questions flooded Stephen's mind as he mopped up the Perrier he'd spilled. Why would someone want to poison me? And who? Did they think a few tainted oysters would drive me out of town? And who was driving the speeding Lexus? Surely it wasn't Taylor, he wouldn't be that obvious. Besides why would he've been in Fairhope the same time Anne and I were having lunch?

"I'm coming," Anne called out as she ran to answer the doorbell.

"I see you're still too stubborn to follow directions," Taylor drawled as Anne peeked through the leaded cut-glass window panes centered in her door.

"Why whatever do you mean?" Anne said, smiling into Taylor's dark brown eyes that matched the leather bomber jacket and brown pants he wore.

Feigning concern, Taylor answered, "I told you not to open this door for anyone."

"Your fancy car roaring up to the curb was a dead give-away. Don't tell me I have you to fear?" she teased as she opened the door.

"Really, now. You know you can trust me. How long have we been friends?"

"For a long time, Taylor," she answered. "Let me help you," she offered, noticing him struggle with four cartons of carryout food and a bottle of wine he carried in his arms. "White zin? You remembered, you're so thoughtful."

Pleased with his foresight, Taylor put the food from the deli on the kitchen table and the wine in the refrigerator. He glanced at Anne's half-stocked shelves and said, "Still a health nut and still flying single, I see."

Taylor liked knowing that she was as alone as his information had indicated. Entering her life might actually be easier than he'd first anticipated. All he had to do was keep her occupied and away from that fool from the East Coast. Smirking slyly, he hoped that Stephen was already packed and on his way to the airport.

"Thanks for coming over," Anne interrupted Taylor's thoughts. "You didn't have to, you know, but I'm glad you're here. I still feel a bit uneasy about that call." She gave him a sisterly hug in appreciation.

Savoring the scent of her hair, Taylor knew he'd made the right decision to stick around Mobile a while longer. Atlanta could wait, something more vital was in the works right now and everything was going his way. He liked being in control.

"What's this pitiful thing?" Taylor asked as he picked up a faded red flower and pulled off one of its few remaining petals.

"Oh, nothing. I guess it does look pretty bad, I really should throw it out." She didn't though. Instead, she took the rose from Taylor's beefy hands, not wanting anyone else to hold the flower Stephen had given her.

"Go on in the living room and I'll get the wine glasses," she said, reaching into the upper cabinet in her small kitchen. After placing the fragile rose carefully inside the cabinet, she found a pretty pair of tulip-shaped antique goblets.

"Fancy glasses," Taylor commented.

"Mother gave them to me when I moved into my first apartment," she explained. Handing him a corkscrew, she said, "If you'd be so kind?"

"My pleasure, ma'am," he replied, pouring out both his charm and the wine. "You sure are a pretty little thing tonight."

Taylor thought how young she looked. "You haven't aged a day since we shared that rum and coke in the stands at the Alabama-Auburn game."

"You haven't changed much either," she said. Then squinting her eyes teasingly, she added, "Maybe you're just a bit larger than you used to be."

"Yeah, and a whole lot richer." Taylor laughed so hard his ample sides shook.

They continued to reminisce about the fun they'd shared during college. Anne felt comfortable with Taylor--he didn't pose any threats to her psyche and he certainly didn't stir her emotions like Stephen had.

Taylor made himself at home and settled deep into Anne's sofa. He half-listened to her talk about her career, her former company, her expansion plans left on the drawing board, and her dream of someday regaining control of Livingston Enterprises. As she talked, he planned. He could see how her sorrow and desires could work to his advantage.

"And, Taylor, the worst is that I didn't see it coming," Anne said with deep remorse and tears in her voice.

"Oh, honey pie, how could you have known? You were so into all the plannin' stages, you just got blind-sided," Taylor consoled her. "Do you have any idea who's actually responsible?"

"No, I don't."

"Well, now," he replied, silently congratulating his behind the scenes team.

She took a deep breath and continued, "Word came that Livingston Enterprises had been acquired by a larger company and contract buyouts were in the works. Then I heard that a group from back East was arriving within days with the paperwork."

"Do you think that guy you were with last night is behind this? You know, there's somethin' about him that sets me off," Taylor said darkly. "What was his name?"

"Stephen? No, I think he came here to do a job and that's all, but he is still in town, so I guess there could be something else going on. I'm really not sure why he decided to stay over."

She thought about Stephen and shivered, remembering when he'd gazed deeply into her eyes. In her heart, she knew that she wanted to be the reason for his change of plans, but reality told her that most likely she had nothing to do with his decision.

Sensing an opportunity to cast doubt in Anne's mind, Taylor inched closer to her on the couch. "Guys like that seem so smooth on the surface. In fact, they're so slick you don't dare turn your back on them. A lot of times those boys turn out to be real chameleons."

Casually resting his arm behind her shoulder, Taylor leaned closer and said, "Suga' foot, you've had a terrible time. But don't you fret, just trust big Taylor. I'll help you with your career. I've got connections all over, we can work somethin' out."

Startled by both Taylor's offer to help and his thinly veiled attack on Stephen, Anne felt suddenly uncomfortable with the nearness of Taylor's large head and mouth. She shifted away from him.

"Why are you being so nice to me?" she asked. "I must look like an incompetent loser to someone as powerful as you. I've heard about your grand successes."

Moving still closer to Anne and breathing into her ear, he whispered, "Now, darlin', you know not to believe half of what you hear. Let's just say I've made a few right choices and some good investments along the way. I am rich, you know, very rich."

Attempting to extricate herself from Taylor's closeness, she rearranged the silverware and china she'd set on their makeshift dinner table in the living room. Taylor, reaching to help her undo the paper food containers, managed to brush his stubby fingers against her forearm.

The more time Taylor spent with Anne, the more satisfied he felt. It wasn't everyday that one could mastermind a takeover of a growing enterprise and walk away with a bonus as well. Yes, he could see Anne as his extra perk in the deal.

With a few changes like a designer wardrobe and a more sophisticated hairstyle, she would make the perfect wife and hostess for a man of his station. Not only was she attractive, she was also polished. Well-versed in business, politics, and the arts, she could converse intelligently with the best. As Anne Hamilton, she would both look good on his arm and fit very nicely in his bed.

Taylor knew, too, that her forgiving nature would give him the space he needed to conduct the licentious activities that were a part of his corporate package. Sometimes he got better tips in the bedroom than the boardroom and that was one part of his life he wasn't about to yield for anyone. Yes, he surmised, finding both Anne and her company in a vulnerable position was a stroke of genius. No one would keep him from closing this deal. She would be his. Nothing would stand in his way.

"Yes, baby doll, I'll circulate your resume to some key people I know. Get me a copy and I'll start things cookin'."

"You're so kind," Anne said, thinking what a nice guy he was to go out of his way to help her. She knew he was important and very busy and she genuinely appreciated the interest he showed in her. Believing he was offering her hope with no strings attached, she felt relieved that their relationship was on a professional basis only.

Mixing business with pleasure had never been her style. Fearing the consequences, she'd always managed to avoid such situations, but all that changed the day temptation in the form of Stephen Richards entered her life. She wondered if she'd ever get him out of her mind.

"You have to watch out for the vipers, little darlin'," Taylor said, reaching for Anne's hand.

She pulled away, saying, "Taylor, I'm sorry, but it's been a long two days for me. I really should get some rest," she added politely, handing him his jacket.

Taylor paused for a moment and then decided against offering to sleep on Anne's couch, just in case she needed protection. "Well, if you're sure you're okay, I'll shove off, for now. But if you should get another of those calls, let me know and I'll head back over."

Pecking Anne's cheek with a cool, emotionless kiss, Taylor walked into the dark, leaving Anne standing by her front door. Turning off the porch light and securing her lock, she went to her bedroom to find Bella.

"Where are you, Bella?" Anne called softly.

She watched Bella crawl cautiously out from underneath the bed. Brushing a small piece of lint from Bella's ear, Anne apologized, "I'm sorry I'm not much of a housekeeper. Unless Taylor saves me from this mess I'm in, I guess I'll have lots of time to push around a dustmop and a broom."

Closing her sleep-filled eyes and snuggling closer against Anne, Bella purred softly.

"Why didn't you come out when Taylor was here? Don't you like him?" she asked. "You've always been a pretty good judge of character. What's the deal now? I think he's one of the good guys. Didn't you hear how he wants to help me? I know, you think I can fix everything all by myself. I used to think no problem was too large for me to handle, but now I'm not so sure."

Anne placed Bella on the edge of her bed and slipped into her pale-blue silky chemise that felt soft and slinky against her skin. She turned down her cotton sheets and crawled into bed. Her thoughts were many as she reflected on her day.

The ride across the Bay, getting rid of Marcie, and being with Stephen had all been fun. The ideas she and Stephen had shared about business research and development had excited her, but the remembered closeness of his firm body next to hers made her feel decidedly warm and very wet. She fantasized about lying beside him. She wondered what his bare chest felt like and if she would dare reach out and caress him all over.

Restless, she got up and went to the kitchen. She stood by the dish-filled sink where she made a promise to herself. Instead of trying to orchestrate every aspect of her life, she would ease off and start listening to her heart.

Then she reached high into the dish cabinet where she'd placed her rose for safekeeping. Finding the flower, she turned out the lights for a second time, returned to bed, and gently tucked the rose underneath her pillow. Peaceful thoughts claimed her as she drifted off to sleep.

CHAPTER 5

Stephen made a paper airplane from a sheet of legal paper and tossed it toward the wastebasket in the corner of the room. "Missed again, bad aim," he said, shaking his head at the mounting stack of yellow missiles that cluttered the floor. He glanced at the clock mounted over the wet bar. It was 4 a.m. and he had little to show for the hours he'd spent tracing Taylor's business history.

He'd placed calls to business associates from Manhattan to Miami and from one end of the Eastern seaboard to the other, he'd heard the same story--Taylor had a reputation as a smooth-talking, aggressive entrepreneur, but his method of operation remained a mystery.

A friend in Boston told Stephen that Taylor possessed vast holdings in the communications industry. How he'd secured the funds to close the deals was a matter of sheer conjecture and wild rumor. Another friend in Charleston ended his conversation with a comment that Stephen didn't really want to hear, "That guy's a powerhouse, a living legend here in Dixieland."

"Powerhouse," Stephen repeated the word through clenched teeth as he dialed another number.

"Matt, Stephen Richards."

"Hey man, what time is it?"

"It's early, sorry, but I need to know something."

"Shoot."

Stephen narrowed his eyes and said, "Tell me what you know about Taylor Hamilton."

"Trying to dig up some dirt?" Matt asked.

"Something like that," Stephen admitted but he didn't elaborate.

"Let's see," Matt answered and then he paused. "I've never met the man but I've heard about him through the grapevine."

"Tell me."

"Had to do with an unfriendly takeover of a small electronics firm in the Silicon Valley."

"What happened?"

"The guy's greased lightening."

"How so?"

"His paper trail ended before the closing documents were signed, but within weeks, the company sold for a major profit and Hamilton's Atlanta bank account reportedly fattened at about the same time."

"Did somebody check it out?" Stephen asked.

"Sure, but the man's smart. Evidently he'd covered his tail so the securities people backed down. He's one tough operator."

Walking to the window, Stephen opened the drapes and saw only darkness. "Communications, electronics, living legend, tough, aggressive," he muttered with disgust. "Calculating, obnoxious, if you ask me."

He called room service and ordered a pot of coffee, saying, "More caffeine, that's what I need." Determined not to give up his pursuit for the truth about Taylor, he rolled up his sleeves and readied himself for an all nighter.

So he's made some bucks here and there, big deal, Stephen thought, he's a lucky weasel, that's all. Thinking about Taylor made Stephen's blood pressure soar. He couldn't stand being around the man and he absolutely could not tolerate Taylor's possessive manner toward Anne.

"Anne!" he said excitedly. "That's it! She's known Taylor longer and better than anyone I've talked to tonight, so of course she must know everything about his past."

He plotted his strategy, debating how to approach his best source of information. He figured Anne was too sharp to be easily fooled so he'd have to make his inquiry appear seemingly innocent, otherwise she'd see right through him.

He thought about calling her right then but changed his mind when he heard someone tap lightly on his door and whisper faintly, "Room service. Coffee, sir."

"Right," Stephen answered as he opened the door and shoved some dollar bills into the server's hand.

He poured a full cup, black, and waited for it to cool. "Think things through, Stephen," he said, as he rubbed his chin. Deciding he needed another shave, he downed his coffee and walked into the bathroom, thinking, I know there's a connection, so I'll find the proof, for Anne.

As he softened his face with shaving creme, he started fantasizing about her for the hundredth time since they'd met. Instead of his hand touching his face, he imagined how soft her fingers would feel. Would her caresses hold the loving, kind emotion that he'd seen in her big blue eyes?

"Dammit," Stephen grumbled, "I just cut myself. Serves me right for mooning over a woman who's probably not giving me a second thought." He pressed at his wound to stop the bleeding, thinking, but why should she? Who am I to her? He rinsed off his razor and reached for a Band-aid.

He stalked around his suite, disappointed that he hadn't been able to uncover more about Taylor. Thirsty for something carbonated, he found some quarters mixed in with his other change and walked down the hall toward the vending machines.

The hallway screamed silence as he made his footsteps light on the jacquard-patterned carpeting. He didn't want to awaken anyone at such an early hour, especially not in a hotel known for its guarantee of providing a good night's rest. Chuckling to himself, he wondered if he could get a refund for the night since he hadn't slept a wink?

He studied his choices at the beverage machine and said, "No sleep for me--more work to do." Dropping his money into the slot, he selected a soda with the highest caffeine content.

He needed a power surge at that moment, but he knew cola wouldn't supply the best stimulus. There was only one power source for him and she was probably sleeping soundly. Picturing Anne in silk and lace, and not too much of that, he took a long, deep drink and returned to his room.

He stretched out on his bed and allowed his mind to drift. He pictured her, lying beside him. Half-dreaming, he could see her face glow as he gently slid the filmy straps of her gown from her shoulders and then carefully lifted it above her head. He sighed as he imagined her closing her eyes and smiling when he tossed her gown aside and nestled her in his arms. He could hear her moan in ecstasy as he stroked her silky hair and kissed her eyelids, first very slowly with his lips and then with his tongue.

"Good God!" he said, his eyes flashing open. He gulped some cola down and held the icy can to his forehead, feeling as though he was on fire and about to explode. Reality verified his feelings as truth because all his physical signs, facial and lower, provided proof positive that an explosion was indeed imminent. He had to find immediate relief. "Fresh, cool air, and fast. I'm out of here," he said, grabbing a jacket and heading for the door.

The sultry night took him by surprise. He quickly pulled off his jacket and let the soft humidity wash over him. Pausing before striking out in a particular direction, he wondered, where to?, it's only 5:30 a.m., the sun's not even up.

He noticed glaring lights a few buildings down from the end of his hotel's parking lot and turned toward a large neon sign that glowed "Cafe du Mobile. Seafood & Sandwiches. Open 24 hours."

The building looked clean, but it was the aroma of hot grease and frying donuts that drew him in. This was his kind of place, inviting, nonassuming, comfortable--an oasis for someone feeling burdened by thoughts for which there was no apparent resolution. For Stephen, this was one of those times.

He'd come to Mobile with a simple agenda: close out an acquisition and get the documents signed in triplicate. Quick, easy, and out the door. Instead, he'd met the boss-- a beautiful, sensitive, intelligent, and very sensuous CEO who was an unwilling party to the transaction.

He recalled the sadness in her eyes, an image that haunted him. Could he have made the changeover less painful for her? He wondered if he should've slowed the whole process, but he hadn't. From past experience, he'd learned that administration transfers worked best when handled rapidly and efficiently. That way all concerned could get on with their lives. No loose ends dangling behind for anyone to trip over.

Stephen sat at the counter and picked up a typed half-page menu. He looked at the words but didn't really read them. Instead, he sorted through the unresolved details in his mind that just didn't compute. He ordinarily knew who was acquiring whom, but this time had been different--a key person hadn't been named as only the initials "TMK" had appeared on the bottom line.

Distracted by other seemingly more difficult assignments, he hadn't inquired as to the particulars of the party his group represented. After all, he'd had no intention of becoming personally involved in what he'd thought was a standard acquisition, a routine buyout of a small company by a source with deep pockets. Yes, he thought, the Livingston file is closed, a done deal. Now, though, he felt riddled with guilt for not having done more homework.

He remembered earlier at the Port O' Call when Anne had listened carefully to his advice about growth potential and capital investments and had said that her greatest wish was to regain control of Livingston Enterprises. Looking into her honest eyes, he'd wanted to reassure her that she stood a chance, but the words hadn't come.

How he wished that he could help her with a battle plan. If only he knew who she might be up against. That missing piece of information drove him crazy.

"Hey, bud, what'll it be?" asked a man wearing a white paper hat twisted sideways across the top of his head and a red apron monogrammed with "Burt" in black thread. "How about an oyster po-boy?"

"No oysters for me but I'll take some coffee, black," Stephen replied, unaware of the edge that'd crept into his voice.

Seeming offended, the man said, "Well then, I guess you won't be needing this." He scooped the menu from Stephen's hand and jammed it into a stand by the cash register.

"Guessed right, pal," Stephen retorted.

"You're the captain," came the curt response from across the counter. "What's eating you anyhow, mister? Problems at home?"

Annoyed, Stephen answered, "Burt, is it? Let me tell you, although it's really none of your business, I don't live here but if I did..."

"Excuse me," Burt interrupted, "I didn't mean anything." Turning his back to Stephen, he mumbled an oath under his breath and poured a mug of coffee. Then he caught a glimpse of Stephen's reflection in the mirror and his manner seemed to soften toward his solitary customer. "A lonely guy," he whispered softly.

Serving Stephen the coffee, he asked, "You want to talk about anything? Most of my customers think I'm a pretty good listener."

Stephen thought for a moment and then decided, why not? "Forgive my bad manners, but I've had some things happen to me here that I didn't expect." And with that Stephen began to talk.

After listening to his story, Burt concluded, "Sounds like you've got more on your mind than business. That little miss you're so worried about seems to have some kind of a hold on you. Now as far as that bag of wind in the sports car goes, why I think you ought to drop him from the picture if he's still in town. Or maybe you're just afraid he's still hanging around."

"Maybe so, Burt. Well, I'd better go get some rest."

"Yep, for the big doin's at Point Clear. I've read about those van Court people in the paper."

"Yes, well, thanks for hearing me out. I'm sorry I acted like a jerk."

"Hey, bud, you're okay." Burt grinned as he placed the money Stephen had left on the counter in the cash register. He watched Stephen walk to the door and said, "All you big guys act tough--until a little missy turns you upside down and inside out. Hope it works out."

"Yeah, right," Stephen called over his shoulder. To himself, he said, "Me, too, but I don't see much hope." He peeled an antacid off the roll of Tums Burt had shoved in his hand with his change.

Wired with caffeine, he walked back to the hotel in record time. Knowing he needed sleep, he wondered if he'd ever rest again.

At his suite, he opened the door and gasped, "What the hell?" Someone had trashed his room, gone through his suitcase and strewn its contents like confetti.

He picked up his legal pad and grimaced. The notes he'd made about Taylor were missing and the sheet of hotel stationery where he'd written Anne's name and phone number had been torn into shreds. "So much for Southern hospitality," he said angrily as he paced back and forth.

Gritting his teeth, he marched to the phone, dialed the front desk, and ordered, "Send security to 904."

"What's wrong, sir?" the clerk asked.

"Get someone up here, now," Stephen barked. Then he slammed down the receiver. He believed he knew who'd done the damage, but he needed proof. Then he thought about Anne, alone and defenseless in her townhome. Concerned for her safety, he wanted to talk with her. He picked up the phone and started to place his call.

"Security, Mr. Richards."

"Come in, the door's open," Stephen replied, miffed that his call to Anne would have to wait as security pummeled him with question after question.

Yes, he'd been absent at the time of entry. And no, he didn't want to move to another suite. Yes, he'd conducted business in town, but no, he didn't think he'd made any enemies.

"No, I can't name anyone who holds ill feelings toward me," he said. Then he thought about the crudely drawn sketch he'd received earlier. Seeing no need to bother security with such a juvenile attempt to run him out of town, he kept mum, for now.

"Morning, Bella, it's about time you got up." Accustomed to rising early for work, Anne'd been awake for hours, had fixed breakfast for both herself and Bella, and now scanned the want ads in the paper. Discouraged that she could find no match for her credentials, she thought of Taylor's offer. Maybe she'd have to take him up on it.

Although she knew she should feel elated that Taylor wanted to help her, she couldn't shake the defeat and sorrow that pained her heart. Maybe I should see a job crisis counselor, she thought. Yes, counseling might be just the ticket, a two for one deal, resume and head exam in one tidy package.

"Oh, Bella, can't you see me describing to a stranger the efficient, well-dressed man who delivered the final takeover papers to my own conference table? Then picture me owning up that I can't get that same man out of my mind. That I'm still waiting for him to call. Geez-o-flip, Bella, imagine all that on somebody's chart."

Then she thought about Stephen's smile, his kindness, his sweet eyes.

"I'm nuts," she said, looking out her front window and chiding herself for being caught up in the moments she and Stephen had shared, few and fleeting though they'd been. Totally blown out of proportion, she thought, deciding Stephen's not calling her proved that he was the kind of guy who did a fast survey of foreign territory, found what was pleasing to his eye, enjoyed it for the moment, and then was on his merry way after his gratification.

"I've been used," she said. "All the warning signs were there. I should've know better." She thought about how many times before she'd met men like Stephen, intelligent, tops of their field, and handsome beyond belief.

But Stephen had seemed different from those other men, he'd appeared to have a kind heart. She thought about the time they'd spent at the Port O' Call when he'd responded so warmly to her hurts and her fears, almost as though he'd known her forever. Not only had he made her feel special, he'd also acted genuinely concerned about her professional future.

When their conversation had hit on her hopes, he'd reassured her that anything was possible, except when she'd talked of one goal in particular--regaining control of her company.

She remembered asking him who was behind the initials on the closing papers. She'd accepted his answer that it was a legitimate company whose credentials were on file with the Securities and Exchange Commission. According to him, all had been on the up and up. But she wondered, was it?

She'd always believed that the other stockholders in the company would've supported her against any potential takeover, especially since she'd sold off her own personal holdings to cover the expansion costs she'd incurred to benefit Livingston Enterprises.

Too bad for her but they hadn't. Instead, the majority controlling block had mandated the transfer of her company into someone else's hands.

She couldn't begin to guess who inside might've turned against her and her family. Surely none of the Livingston employees could've been swayed by someone's checkbook. On that, she would bet her life.

Anne turned off her coffeemaker and grabbed a dishtowel to clean up the drips she'd left on the kitchen countertop. Walking by her telephone mounted on the wall by the refrigerator, she glared at it and said, "Oh, Stephen, why did I dream about you calling? You really don't care about me, do you? Why did I think you were different? I must've been crazy, stupid, or both."

Then she thought about Taylor. At least he seemed to understand her situation and want to do something to make it better.

Upset, she reached to refill her coffee cup, but the sudden ringing of the phone made her drop it in the sink.

"Hello?" she answered.

"Anne?"

"Stephen?"

"Yes, it's me. Are you all right?"

"Sure, I'm fine," she answered, wondering why he sounded somewhat agitated.

"I haven't been able to get you off of my mind."

"Is that so?" she said, thinking, if you'd really cared, you'd have called me before now.

"You don't sound fine to me. What's going on? Is there something you're not telling?"

"Actually, yes, someone left a threatening message on my answering machine, but my friend Taylor Hamilton--do you remember him from the other night?--came right on over and I've been perfectly all right ever since."

"Taylor Hamilton to the rescue? Really?" he asked, hating that Taylor had been Anne's saving knight. Damn, he thought, I spent all night trying to find out the truth about that snake. For what? The man's a saint in her eyes.

"Stephen, it's really no big deal."

"What do you mean, Anne? What was said?" Stephen asked.

"It's dumb to talk about this. Besides, the caller probably had the wrong number."

"What was said?" Stephen persisted.

"That I should stay with my own kind."

"Stay with your own kind? Anne, don't you get it? The caller's telling you to stay away from me."

"You? Why? Stephen, that's ridiculous. Who would care? Besides, our relationship is only business anyhow and since my business is now dead, what's the deal?"

"I'm not sure what's going on but things are not as they seem."

"Look, I haven't gotten any other calls, so I think it's all a moot point. So, tell me, why are you calling?"

Stephen decided against sharing his past hours with Anne. All of the craziness he'd encountered made no sense to him, so why should it to her? He cursed the circumstances that'd kept him from calling her. Worrying that she probably believed he was a common, insensitive lout, he determined he'd show her differently.

"Well then, I guess since your pal Taylor takes such excellent care of your safety, all that's left for me to do is stand around with my hands in my pockets."

She caught her breath as she remembered seeing Stephen stuff his hands in his khakis when they'd stood side by side and thigh to thigh in Fairhope. Recalling his reaction to her, aroused and ready, she sighed, "Oh, Stephen."

"What is it?"

"Nothing, I suppose you're calling about the van Courts' dinner?"

He wanted to say, "No, I'm calling to tell you that I care about you and I fear there's been some deceit in your business life," but he thought better and said instead, "Yes, let's firm up our plans."

"Do you want me to drive?" she asked.

"No," he answered, "I will."

"Okay, but do you remember where I live?"

"Yes, Anne, my memory span actually lasts longer than two days. So give me a time and I'll be there," he answered, hoping she'd invite him over a few hours earlier.

"Mrs. van Court hasn't called yet but cocktails are usually at six and since it's about a forty minute drive, you can figure out the math," she replied matter-of-factly, trying to disguise the anticipation she felt.

"Well then, Miss Livingston. It's a date. Will you be ready when I call?"

"But of course," she replied lightly although she really wondered if she spoke the truth.

CHAPTER 6

Looking at the mountainous mass of tangled hangers and rumpled clothing piled on her bed, Anne searched under the stack for Bella who'd found a soft hiding place. "Peek-a-boo, baby," she teased, laughing at the comical, puzzled look on her cat's pretty face.

Bella peeped out from beneath a cocktail dress fashioned from lemon-ice chiffon and satin. "Is that your choice?" Anne asked, tilting her head to one side.

Bella placed a furry paw on the beaded bodice as if to say, "This one, for sure."

Anne had spent hours trying on clothes. Thinking, this can't be me, she remembered all the afternoons she'd delegated assignments and studied marketing plans. Now, without makeup and with her hair twisted around pink velcro rollers that looked like pipelines, she said, "What a difference a few days can make." Frustrated, she shook her head and jarred one of the rollers loose.

Bella lunged for it as it bounced on the hardwood floor and rolled. Capturing it for a moment, she gnawed at her new toy and then batted it under the bed.

Bending over, Anne retrieved the roller with her right hand and grabbed Bella with her left. Fondly placing Bella on her dressing table bench, she stood by her mirror. She reached for her shimmery dress, held it up, and said, "You're right, this is the one."

The phone rang and the doorbell chimed at the same time, setting both Anne and her cat into full motion. "Who can that be?" Anne muttered as she slipped on her robe and walked toward the living room. "I'm coming. Just a minute."

She breezed past her ringing phone and paused to switch on her answering machine to pick up the call. Hearing her greeting play but not a following message, she opened her front door.

"Hi," she said, smiling at a delivery boy who carried a rectangular white box tied with a bright red ribbon. She felt suddenly self-conscious when she watched the boy's eyes rove from her top to her bottom and then glance away. Realizing how she must appear in her robe and rollers, she blushed.

"Miss Livingston, this is for you," he said with a broad grin as he handed her the box and walked back to his truck.

Anne studied the delivery card as she closed her door. Since she didn't recognize the handwriting and still felt uneasy from her mystery phone call, she carefully opened the box. One look and she sighed with pleasure.

"Beautiful," she said, admiring a delicate corsage of white gardenias. "So heavenly," she added, bending forward to sample their sweet fragrance.

She moved the flowers aside and picked up a small enclosure card. "How thoughtful," she said, as she slowly took in the message--"Looking forward to tonight. Yours, Stephen."

Wondering if she'd been too harsh in her judgment of him, she smiled. Then thinking the flowers might be his way of softening her up so he could better network her friends, she frowned. "Whatever," she said, tossing her head high. "I really don't care, I'll just enjoy them." She touched a soft white petal before closing the flowers up and placing them in the refrigerator for safekeeping. "What a guy," she said.

Then she noticed her message light flashing and assumed he'd called, probably to see if she'd received the flowers. Expecting to hear his voice, she pushed the play button and listened.

"'lo, darlin'. It's just me, Taylor. Where are you, sweetie? Can't have wandered far. Listen here, I was serious about sendin' your resume around, so give me a buzz on my car phone--I left you the number. Better yet, I'll just spin on by. And if you're a good little puss, I'll buy you another dinner. Later, baby."

"Taylor, Taylor," she said with a bemused laugh as she picked up her phone to return his call. Ordinarily, she would've found his language and attitude sexist, offensive, and most annoying, but she considered the source and rationalized his manner as "just his way."

She remembered their college days when many of her sorority sisters had begged her to fix them up with the dashing and seemingly destined for riches Taylor Hamilton. She'd often wondered why most of those women seemed to change their minds about him after one date. At the time, though, she'd been so wrapped up in her own failed relationship that she hadn't kept up with the house gossip.

Recalling that Taylor'd always maintained that he was the cautious, selective type, a man who planned to stay single until he found the woman of his dreams, she figured that none of her sisters had been really right for him.

So be it, she thought, all the while feeling secure in her friendship with him. She didn't worry that maybe he had eyes for her. They simply enjoyed each other's company, that was the sole extent of their involvement, at least, that's what she thought.

Thinking, a relationship is the last complication I need in my life right now, she dialed Taylor's number, hoping to catch him in time. She didn't want him to waste a trip.

"Hello, Taylor? This is Anne. I'm sorry I missed your call."

"Oh, suga' pie, that's all right. I'm on Cottage Hill and comin' your way. So spruce up your resume and pick out somethin' pretty to wear. How's the Malaga Inn sound for dinin' and dealin'? We can talk about your qualifications over a pitcher or two of sangria. How about it, babe?" He paused and grinned slyly as he thought about her credentials: sweet, bright enough, a woman with potential just waiting to be molded.

"I'm sorry, Taylor, but I've already made some other plans."

"You're turnin' big Taylor down? What's goin' on? You sneak a stud in your stable?" The smile drained from his face.

"Heavens no, Taylor. It's just that I'm having dinner with...." she paused and then hurriedly added, "my grandfather. You probably haven't heard, but he hasn't been feeling too well so I need to spend some time with him."

He sensed that she wasn't telling the whole truth but then he decided to let it pass. "Although I'm jealous as hell, I respect your family loyalty. Eh, kissy face, you go on and do what you think's right."

"I'll see you another time," Anne replied, breathing a deep sigh of relief.

"Sure, and give my regards to Mr. Livingston. Tell him I said he's a lucky gent to get to share your company. By the way, how'd he take the news about the business?"

"I haven't told him much, he's been so sick. But when he's stronger, I plan to fill him in on the details. You know how many questions he'll have."

"Well, kitty cat, if anyone can find the right words, it'll be you. But if I can help, just say so and we'll get our heads together, real soon."

Thinking, what a nice guy, she said, "Thanks for understanding. I promise we'll make plans later on."

Hanging up, she turned away from her phone and kneeled beside Bella who'd come looking for attention. As she rubbed Bella's ears, she worried, What have I done now? I shouldn't have hedged the truth. Everytime I fib I get caught. What if Taylor should see me with Stephen? Or if he drives by my grandfather's house and decides to stop in, then he'll know that I lied to him.

"I should've told the truth," she said as she watched Bella turn, stretch, and prance away. Muttering, "This is just wonderful, now I even have my cat's disapproval," she stood up, walked to her dressing table, and reached for her favorite perfume.

"Who's she talking to?" a frustrated Stephen grumbled into his phone before putting it down for the seventh time in the past ten minutes. "Wonder if she's on the line with that puffed up, sanctimonious Taylor Hamilton?" Thinking about him monopolizing Anne's time brought thoughts of dueling to Stephen's tortured mind.

Still seething with anger, he growled, "What now?" when someone knocked on his door politely at first and then more persistently. Ready to battle, he threw the door wide open.

Standing in the hallway was a young man about fifteen wearing red high-tops that matched his flaming red hair and rosy cheeks. "Excuse me, Mr. Richards. I brought your suit from the Magic Touch Pressers," he explained as he handed over the finely tailored garment.

Stephen reached into his pocket and paid the cleaning charge along with a bonus, saying, "Here you go, thanks."

"Oh sir, thank you," the boy replied as he carefully counted the money. "I really appreciate this and hope you have a good evening."

Stephen closed the door and said under his breath, "That makes two of us, son." Good kid, he thought, recognizing some of himself in the boy. He knew the difficulties of juggling school and home responsibilities with part-time jobs. He'd held several himself--yardwork, paper routes, flipping burgers, he'd done them all.

Not from the privileged background of people like Taylor, Stephen believed he'd benefited from having to work hard his whole life because he'd learned firsthand what it took to be successful. Somehow guys like Taylor never seemed satisfied with what they had--they always pressed for more, sometimes tripping themselves up along the way. He wondered about Taylor's methods, his connections. Were they on the up and up?

Noticing the time, he began to dress for the evening but the excitement he felt made it difficult for him to get everything together. "Where are my socks?" he fumed. "Damn button," he cursed, after accidentally ripping one from the front of his starched, white dress shirt. Finding another shirt that would have to make do, he paused to look at himself in the mirror. "Come on, Richards, what is it with you? You've been to hundreds of these dinners--this is just one more."

Shaking his head, he thought, Who am I kidding? It's not the dinner, it's Anne--I can't wait to see her. Then he pictured her preparing for their evening out. When he imagined her slipping silk stockings over her shapely legs and then higher, he had to sit down. "She's driving me nuts," he muttered as he pulled on yet another pair of mismatched socks.

* * * *

Anne, freshly bathed and moisturized from her forehead to her toes, prepared to dress for her date with Stephen. Slipping her dress carefully over her head, she moved her shoulders slightly to help slide the tight-fitting skirt over her toned body.

"I like this dress," she said, zipping it up easily.

Looking at her image in the mirror, she smiled, happy with what she saw. A perfect fit and her hair glistened in the warm light cast from the lamp by her bed.

She completed her makeup with a flick of her mascara wand, a fine coat of translucent powder, and a light brush of pale lipstick. Blotting her lips with a tissue, she noticed the pinkish outlines left behind. "Look, Bella, little kisses all in a row," she said. Then an image flashed in her mind, causing her to blush crimson. She'd seen herself starting a trail of kisses at the base of Stephen's ear, slowly marching them down his chest, and only stopping when she reached...

"I'm just going out of my mind--too much pressure lately, that's it." Regaining her composure, she thought, besides, he's not interested in me. "Better keep it light, Anne," she instructed herself as she slipped on ivory satin heels that complemented her dress. She twirled around twice and smiled. Maybe we'll dance tonight, she thought.

She searched for her white gloves and evening bag in the top drawer of her dresser. Finding them where she'd stored them five years ago, she checked them and thought, no holes or mildew, that's good. Then she listened for footsteps on her walk. Unable to resist the urge, she spritzed on one last bit of perfume and walked to the door and waited.

Filled with anticipation, she felt her heart pound and her body warm. Powerless to control the tingling that coursed through her fingertips and the warmth that blossomed in the core of her womanhood, she rode with her feelings. A woman she definitely was, a woman whose femininity had been untouched for far too long.

Stephen straightened his Countess Mara tie and brushed back his hair that'd fallen rakishly over his forehead. He could see Anne waiting inside and his heart raced. Through the center pane of glass, he saw her, dressed to the nines. When she turned slightly sideways, he caught his breath-- her perfect body, gorgeous, he thought, as desire raced through him.

When she suddenly stretched her hands to the top of her head and tousled her hair so it rippled and waved down her back, he caught his breath. He watched as she bent over and shook her head from side to side. The motion of her hair and the movement of her full breasts mesmerized him to the point that he could barely put one foot in front of the other.

Stephen cleared his dry throat and made his way up the steps to her door. He knocked five times and waited for Anne to welcome him in. He pushed all of his cares from his mind and concentrated solely on the most perfect woman he'd ever seen.

"Anne, you leave me breathless." He heard the words come from his mouth but he had no knowledge of forming them. Taking her hands in his, he pulled her close to him. Her intoxicating scent overcame him as he felt himself falling captive to her spell.

She pulled back at first, but then she succumbed to the power of his embrace. She yielded heart and soul to the overwhelming strength of his body as he made no sign of releasing her. She didn't want him to let her go.

With his left hand, he lifted her chin and carefully turned her beautiful head in such a way that he could bend down to taste the nectar of her lips. Ever so gently, he kissed her deeply, setting her on fire and making her crave more. He parted her lips slightly and gently met her tongue with his. He felt her stiffen in surprise, but then she responded as he probed the recesses of her mouth deeper and deeper.

Holding her as though there was no tomorrow, he allowed his body to show her exactly how desirable he found her.

Hers echoed his need and there was no stopping their kisses as they gave loving sweetness, one to the other.

Finally pulling away, Anne looked at Stephen and with wide-eyed innocence asked, "Good God, is this how you start all your dates?"

"I couldn't help myself. You are without a doubt the most exquisite woman I've ever seen," he answered with stars shining in his deep blue eyes.

Feeling her cheeks redden, Anne tried to stop the glow she felt spreading across her face. "Do you really expect me to fall for that line, Stephen Richards?"

"I'm a truthful man. Come here and let me show you some more honesty," he challenged.

Not about to back down from his dare, she moved closer to Stephen who quickly placed his hands around her small waist and pulled her up tightly against his chest. As he did, he looked straight into her eyes and locked his gaze with hers.

She felt her breath catch in her throat when he worshipped her with his eyes. Believing that she'd just witnessed his burning desire pass from his body into hers, she shuddered, sensing his passion.

Unable to trust himself with Anne any further, he kissed her softly and let her go. Although the throbbing he felt in his manhood approached the maximum pain threshold, he knew that she was far too precious to frighten away with his need. Even so, though, he'd seen her passionate side and he knew he'd awakened her spirit, her fire.

He decided he'd wait to make Anne his, he'd let her tell him when the time was right. Whenever she was ready, he would be there to give her all the love she could handle. He'd never wanted a woman as much as he desired Anne.

Stunned by how lightheaded she suddenly felt, Anne whispered, "I think we probably should go now if we're going to make the van Courts' dinner."

"Whatever you say, Anne. Tell me what you want and I'll do your bidding."

"It's time, Stephen," she answered dreamily.

"Lead the way and I'll follow, princess."

Before locking her front door, Anne remembered that she needed to check her answering machine.

"Why?" he asked. "It's after work hours. Are you expecting a call?"

"No, but my grandfather or one of his neighbors might need to reach me, so I like to leave it on, just in case," she explained. As she spoke, she recalled the memory of the threatening message she'd received and shivered at the coldness of the warning she'd heard.

Becoming attuned to her mannerisms, Stephen put his arm protectively around her shoulder and said, "Something's bothering you but I won't pry. Just know that I'm ready to listen."

Smiling softly, she latched the deadbolt lock and they began their drive to Point Clear. As they passed through the small towns of Daphne, Montrose, and Fairhope, they talked about their pasts.

She discovered that he was from a large, old New England family and that he respected his parents, their values, and the solid foundation they'd given him. She learned, too, that he'd worked his way through Haverford College and Penn's Wharton School of Finance. Watching his eyes soften when he told her how he drew strength from memories of his family whenever times got tough, she felt her heart go out to him.

He seemed so open to her questions that she decided to inquire about his personal life.

Stephen glanced down and said, "That's more than enough about me, so tell me about you."

He learned of her deep Southern roots, her background of private schools and Pony Club meets, her love for her parents and her brother, her closeness to her grandfather, her humiliation at losing control of their dynasty, and her college romance.

"Did you learn anything from having lost at love?"

"Yes, to keep things simple and never to trust my heart to anyone again," she answered firmly and then added, "regardless how good-looking and exciting that anyone might be."

Stephen nodded his head and agreed, "We learned the same lesson. Guess that's why we're still single."

Silence commanded their car as they reflected on all they'd just shared with each other, but their private reveries came to a sudden stop.

A pair of flashing bright lights almost blinded Stephen when he looked in the rear view mirror, causing him to shout, "What's that fool behind me up to?"

Suddenly the other car surged forward with its horn blaring wildly and seemed headed right for Stephen and Anne.

She screamed when she felt their car run off the shoulder of the narrow and dimly lit back road.

"Hold on," Stephen said, shoving the gearshift into overdrive and cutting the front wheels sharply toward the pavement. He didn't really know any high speed driving skills, but on this night he could've challenged the best racer in the land. He urged his car forward, demanding all its engine could give.

Thinking they were out of danger, he relaxed, only to tense again when he saw the beaming headlights gaining on them. He gritted his teeth and kept his concentration focused as he skillfully outmaneuvered the dark car.

"If this idiot wants a challenge, I'll give him full measure," Stephen said, glaring into his side mirror as he gunned his engine and roared ahead.

Although he thought he recognized both the car and its driver, he kept his suspicions to himself. He didn't want to alarm Anne, but now he believed for sure that she was definitely keeping dangerous company and the man from the North sitting beside her was not the problem.

Anne pondered the last five minutes, her tense body language signaling the fear and worry that raced through her mind--What on earth is going on here? Why would someone want to run us off the road? Maybe whoever called me was serious. Maybe it wasn't a wrong number after all.

Stephen felt his thoughts connect with hers. He knew that the mild breezes outside could turn to hurricane force winds in a heartbeat and that was precisely what he wanted to shelter Anne from. She'd already endured enough turmoil in her life and this latest intrusion wasn't necessary. He'd find the culprit and make him pay--he'd see to that before he left town, even if the beast should prove to be Anne's trusted friend, Taylor Hamilton.

CHAPTER 7

Stephen and Anne passed through the stone-pillared front gate of the Grand Hotel at Point Clear. Still unnerved by the reckless driver who'd almost caused them to crash, Anne asked rather shakily, "Do you believe in bad omens?"

"Not really," he answered, noticing that her breathing seemed almost normal.

"What about rewards for surviving horrible ordeals?"

He smiled and said, "Now that's a much better concept."

"I agree," she replied. She thought for a moment and then suggested, "Maybe since we made it through that scare on the road, we're destined for a great time tonight."

Stephen noticed the lack of color in her cheeks and realized that she was still frightened. That was when he decided that he'd become her protector, her shield, at least for tonight.

"Do you think this will be an evening to remember?" she asked.

He smiled and replied, "Let's plan on it. You can trust me to make it happen."

She looked at him warily, not realizing that her eyes spoke volumes. Although a part of her wanted to trust him 100%, the rest of her waved a caution flag.

He sensed her feelings and didn't blame her for her mistrust. He knew the acquisition had taken its toll, but he wondered if she'd always be suspicious of everyone connected with the deal, even those without the initials "TMK."

"Something bothering you?" he asked as they coasted to a stop at the end of the brick-paved drive.

"No, it's nothing, really," she answered and then looked away. She remembered when her worries only concerned her professional life but now she felt uneasy about her personal safety, as well.

"Come on, spill it," he encouraged, not liking the distance he felt growing between them.

Sighing, she said, "I was just thinking about the last few days and about what lies ahead." She came within a breath of telling him the extent of her fears, but then she pulled back, deciding not to involve him in her problems.

"I understand," he said. "But maybe there's a silver lining out there somewhere."

"I wish, but I doubt it," she replied, gazing out the window. She shivered at the memory of the mysterious phone call she'd received. Then she recalled when she'd been in the Page & Palette and had felt secret, strange eyes spying on her. She thought, too, about the crazed driver who'd terrified her to her soul only minutes ago. Who and why? Isolated events or a pattern? And what else?

Searching for answers and finding none, she turned her attention to Stephen, who asked, "Are you settled enough to go inside?"

"Ready and willing," she answered, causing Stephen's eyes to gleam.

He whistled at his thoughts and waited for the valet to take his keys. Gently assisting Anne from the car, he took her by the hand and led her to the edge of the lush lawn. "Let's sit for a minute," he said, nodding toward a cypress bench. "I want to soak up some of this ambiance before we go inside."

After minutes of shared silence, he turned to her and said, "I've traveled from coast to coast and I've seen a world of beautiful sights, but I swear, for the life of me, I can't think of a grander place than right here."

"It is pretty spectacular," she agreed with a touch of pride in her voice.

"Look at that hotel--it's an architectural prize," he said, thinking about the article he'd read in the tourist magazine. "I saw an aerial photo that showed why Point Clear came by its name but it didn't come close to capturing all this majesty, this splendor. A palace with a marina, golf course, tennis courts, and bowling greens, to boot. Incredible!"

Standing up, he motioned for Anne to follow. "Come here, you've got to see this." In the soft glow of the evening shadows, he pointed toward the hotel that seemed to soar into the lights of the sky.

"Worth the drive?" she asked.

"Definitely!" he exclaimed. He glanced back at row after row of moss-draped trees that lined the drives of the parking areas. He wondered what stories those live oaks could tell.

"Is that all you have to say?" she asked as disappointment clouded her face.

"Oh, Anne, I wish I were a poet so I could put on paper the way I feel right now." The combination of Point Clear's charm and Anne's sensuality delivered a powerful blow to his heart. He breathed deeply as he took in all that surrounded him, thankful that he was alive.

"Happy?" she asked.

"Beyond my wildest dream."

"Surprised?"

"Pleasantly," he replied, ashamed for the way he'd reacted when given his assignment to South Alabama. He remembered scoffing to his team that they probably wouldn't have any trouble making overnight reservations since no one ever came to Mobile.

"If you like what you see here, you'll have to drive to the Gulf. It's not far," Anne said. "I think you'll love it," she added with a coy wink.

"Are you offering to take me to paradise?" he asked, thinking he was already there.

She avoided his question by asking one of her own. "Now do you understand why I don't want to move away from here?"

"I think so," he answered, "especially since you're a born and bred woman of the New South."

"Why, Stephen Richards, I think you're making fun of me. Are you?"

He took her right hand and planted a kiss on her fingertips.

"Well?" she prodded.

"Never, Anne, but I do worry about your trusting nature."

"What do you mean?"

"Your friends, like...," he said, pausing as he looked down.

"Taylor?" she asked, feeling suddenly defensive.

"Yes, him," he answered, tasting bile rise in his throat at the mention of the man's name.

Anne placed her hands on her hips and lectured, "My friends are important to me, especially old friends and..."

Tempted to tease her about the way she'd greeted her old friend Marcie, Stephen thought better and kept quiet, letting her continue.

"...and that's what makes friendships special--they endure and transcend time."

"Right," he said as he stood up and checked his watch. "Is it time for us to go inside?"

"Yes, if you promise to be nice to all my friends."

"Whatever you say," he answered as he escorted her toward the main dining room.

"Anne, where have you been?" Mrs. van Court said, leaving her other guests in mid-conversation. "We were beginning to worry about you--and your friend, of course." She hugged Anne and when Anne trembled slightly, she suggested, "Let's find a quiet place so we can visit for a while." She led Anne to a settee in the foyer and signaled a waiter to serve them wine.

After greeting Mr. van Court, Stephen positioned himself near Anne. He listened to her retell the horror of their drive over the road she'd said usually provided only a scenic view. He wished that had been his experience.

"I can't believe that someone tried to hurt us intentionally," she said. "Whenever we sped up, so did the other car and when we slowed, it did, too. Every time I glanced in the mirror, all I saw were high beams aimed straight for us."

Hearing bits and pieces of Anne's story, Mr. van Court asked Stephen if he got the license number.

"No sir, I couldn't see the plate and it happened so fast that I'm not positive about the make of the car either. It took all I had to keep us on the road. Thank God, Anne warned me about the twists and turns, she literally..."

"Oh, Stephen, tell the truth," Anne interrupted. "You know that I closed my eyes in sheer panic."

"That's not the way I remember it," Stephen said. He wanted to say more but his attention shifted suddenly toward the portico facing the Bay when he heard a booming voice yell, "Hot damn! It's party time."

"Oh my gosh!" Anne said, her glance following Stephen's. Her eyes locked with those of Taylor Hamilton.

Taylor raised a glass of champagne as though he was making a toast and bowed his head in Anne's direction.

"Anne, isn't that your friend, uh, what's his name? Taylor? Taylor Hamilton?" Mrs. van Court asked.

"Oh, yes. That's Taylor," Anne answered. Under her breath, she added, "I should've told the truth. Damn, double damn."

"Excuse me?" Stephen said.

"You wouldn't understand, Stephen. I messed up and now I feel like an idiot."

"What are you talking about?"

"Taylor's a great guy and he's offered to help me find another job."

"So?"

Upset, she struggled to explain, "It's dumb but I didn't want to tell him that you and I were going out tonight, so instead, I kind of told him I'd be with my grandfather. And now, he's here and--oh my, no, he's coming this way."

"Great. Such a swell fellow," Stephen muttered as he watched Taylor work the room on his way over to where he stood with Anne.

"You're lookin' pretty tonight, Anne, but isn't Point Clear a bit out of your way? Savin' room for a midnight supper?" He gave Anne a look that made her wilt and then he turned toward Stephen, extended his hand, and said, "Good to see you, again, uh, Steve, wasn't it? I didn't know you were still hangin' around."

"Yes, I decided to extend my stay," Stephen replied, extricating his hand from the bone-crushing clasp of Taylor's cold hand.

Staring at Stephen with narrow, grey eyes, Taylor hissed so that only Stephen could hear, "Don't get too comfortable. Southern hospitality only stretches so far, and if visitors overstay their welcome, we have a way of movin' 'em on."

"Is that a threat?" Stephen asked, towering his 6'2" frame over the shorter Taylor.

"No, hoss, that's a promise," Taylor said, turning on his heels and rejoining his party that'd moved to an outside pavilion.

"What was that all about?" Anne asked.

"Just one of your old pals who transcends time," Stephen answered without smiling.

"Did he say something to upset you?" she asked.

"No, he only wanted to wish me a safe bon voyage." Stephen turned to meet the van Courts' other guests who'd been enjoying cocktails and the evening breeze on a veranda adjacent to the dining room.

Satiated with hors d'ouevres of shrimp puffs and crabmeat supreme, the party made their way inside and found their places at a table set for twelve in the middle of the dining room.

"Pretty," Stephen said, as Anne toyed with a tri-color streamer of ribbon that decorated her placecard.

"Mardi Gras balls in Mobile start next week," she explained. "These are the carnival colors--purple, green, and gold. They'll be on every street corner downtown from now until Lent."

Stephen nodded, thinking about the Mardi Gras season he'd spent in New Orleans years ago. He recalled that his celebration had gotten way out of hand and now all he could remember was a pounding headache that'd lasted a month and a sympathetic blond who'd kept him company until he'd run out of money. That hadn't been a good time in his life.

He'd gone there on the rebound from a relationship that should never have been. The president of an industrial com-

plex had admired his proficiency at overseeing a compli-
cated international deal. As a result, he'd not only entrusted
Stephen with a $20 million contract, he'd also encouraged
him to romance his daughter, India. At odds from day one,
Stephen and India had parted soon after on less than amica-
ble terms, causing Stephen to shun personal involvements
spawned by business connections.

"Stephen, your place is next to Brandie Sue," Mrs. van
Court said, drawing him back into the present.

He sat down and nodded politely to his dinner partner,
a vivacious young woman with raven black hair.

Seeming delighted to have Stephen seated by her side,
Brandie Sue emoted and performed as though she was on
stage at the Saenger Theatre. From the time of the host's
dinner toast through the clearing of the salad plates, she
talked non-stop about Mardi Gras, Mobile style.

Unaware that Mobile was the birthplace of Mardi Gras
in America, Stephen listened intently as Brandie Sue explained the importance of observing strict protocol at the
formal society balls that kept all of the Port City dancing
for days and nights.

Although her dark beauty would ordinarily have capti-
vated most men, Stephen seemed oblivious to Brandie Sue's
charms. He couldn't keep his eyes off of Anne--and her
dinner partner, Dr. Scott Du Maurier, a handsome internist.

Stephen tried to maintain his cool, but he felt his stomach
knot when he watched Anne smile at the doctor whose whispered words seemed to delight her.

Tapping on Stephen's arm, Brandie Sue leaned toward
him and said, "Scott was named Bachelor of the Year by
the Spinsters Society at their annual ball. He's a real catch."

Every so often, Stephen stole a few quick glances from
Anne, but they were fleeting as Scott, who obviously was no
one's fool, seemed quite taken with Anne's sexy sweetness.

"Pay attention to me," Brandie Sue said with a charming
pout, but Stephen couldn't. He was too entranced with the
scene playing in front of his eyes.

Unable to endure seeing Anne's head touching Scott's as
they discussed the merits of blackened fish, he broke up

their conversation by asking, "Anne, what did you tell me was the difference between Creole and Carolina gumbo?"

Shooting him a look that said "I can't believe what you just asked," she replied, "Are you talking about okra, Stephen?"

"Yeah, that slimy stuff," he muttered and then realizing how foolish he must appear, he hurriedly explained to the other guests, "Forgive me, but I'm intrigued by local customs." He spent the rest of the six course dinner in silence.

Brandie Sue, seemingly drawn by Stephen's aloofness, moved closer to him and asked, "Did I tell you about the colors that decorate all the King Cakes I'm sure you've seen? Well, the purple's for justice, green's for faith, and gold stands for power." She gazed into his eyes and placed her small bejeweled hand on his sleeve. Whispering so only he could hear, she said, "I'll bet gold's your favorite of the three since I'm sure you understand power more than anyone else in this whole room."

He coughed nervously, wanting desperately to escape Brandie Sue's unwanted attention without offending her. Patting her hand in a fatherly way, he smiled and said, "If you'll excuse me for a minute, I need to have a private word with Anne."

Brandie Sue crossed her arms over her full bosom and huffed, "That's fine with me but you're too late, see, there she goes outside with Scott. Geez, they didn't even wait for dessert." She lowered her long eyelashes over her doe-like eyes and said, almost purring, "So, I guess you'll just have to have your private word with me."

Catching a glimpse of sparkling beads and lemon-ice satin passing through the French doors that led to a garden, Stephen conceded that Brandie Sue was right--Anne indeed had left him to fend for himself. He turned to the others, hoping to start a conversation with someone other than Brandie Sue, but he only received polite nods as the remaining guests followed Anne and Scott's lead by excusing themselves to "walk off dinner," "grab a smoke," or "freshen up before dessert."

Alone with Stephen, Brandie Sue acted as though she'd just won the Florida lottery. "Now, Stephen, what do you want to talk about?"

"Okay, Brandie Sue, tell me how well you know Anne," he replied, trying to salvage this part of his evening. Maybe she could give him some answers to the questions he had.

Seeming disappointed that he appeared only concerned about Anne, Brandie Sue pouted for a moment but then she said with a laugh, "Anne Livingston as an ice breaker, she'd die at the thought."

"So what do you know?" he asked.

"Let's see, we've been friends since junior high. We both went to UMS-Wright Prep and the same church, so I guess you could say we've known each other for a pretty long time."

"What was she like then?"

Brandie Sue stroked the stem of her wine glass and then answered, "I'm not sure I understand what you really want to know, but she's always been kind of driven, really focused on her career, success, you know, things like that. That's probably why she and Taylor have been friends since middle school--they're a lot alike, you know."

"I thought they met at college." Stephen tried to cover the scowl in his voice. The idea that Anne had known Taylor since childhood and, even worse still, respected him made Stephen's blood boil. He clenched his fist in anger, hating that Anne couldn't see Taylor Hamilton the way he did-- arrogant, pompous, self-serving.

Brandie Sue, watching the veins in Stephen's temples throb, sighed heatedly. She fanned herself with a napkin and angled her body so that he had a clear view of her cleavage. "Forget Taylor," she said, "you're my kind of man."

"Pardon?" Stephen said, looking frantically around the room for Anne.

"Men like you are hard to find. I'm going to send Mrs. van Court flowers for putting us together."

"Excuse me, Brandie Sue, I don't want you to get the wrong idea, but..."

"No buts, Stephen. Looks like we were destined to be together. Anne's off with the Doc so it's just you and me, Mr. Handsome."

"Now about Taylor and Anne..." Stephen said as he disengaged his thigh from Brandie Sue's hand that massaged muscles he didn't know he had.

"Didn't you see the way Taylor looked at her? That says it all, I think," she answered testily.

Stephen grimaced at the memory of Taylor leering at Anne, appraising her from top to bottom and back again. He gritted his teeth, almost forcing steam to come out of his ears. Coldly, he said, "Yes, I couldn't miss the sexist, condescending manner of your friend."

"Wait a minute, who said he was my friend?" she protested. "He's Anne's. Surely you saw the way she drew him from way across the room, why, she must've given him a special look--he ran right over like a bird dog after quail. What do you think he meant about a midnight supper? Maybe they've set a late date?" Brandie Sue teased.

"Impossible, Anne wouldn't consider such a thing," Stephen replied frostily.

"Oh really?" Brandie Sue said with a smug smile. "Taylor has a way of getting people to do what he wants. I know that for a fact."

"What happened?"

"He told me he loved me, but it didn't last."

"Oh, that's too bad," Stephen sympathized.

"Not really, neither of us was thinking about a long-term commitment. We were at the Azalea Ball, having the time of our life, dancing under the stars as the band played on and on."

"I see."

"He wanted me, and I..., well, we ended up in his family's cottage on Plash Island."

"He took advantage of you, your innocence?"

"Let's not talk about that, but I'll tell you one thing. He may have some faults, but he's not as bad as some people around here think. In fact, I believe most of the rumors are just mean-spirited gossip."

"Like what?" Stephen felt as though he was finally getting somewhere.

"Oh--that he's rich, and because he's young, he had to have gotten all that money by questionable means. Then there's his sex life."

"What are you saying, Brandie Sue?" Stephen probed.

"Taylor comes and goes a lot. Atlanta's his home base now, but he spends some time here and when he does, most men want to lock up their women, if you know what I mean," she said with a touch of wickedness in her voice. "He is pretty amazing," she added with a knowing smile.

Not liking the turn of their conversation, Stephen tried to shift Brandie Sue's thoughts away from Taylor the lover to Taylor the businessman. "What kind of business is Taylor's?"

"I'm not really sure. He's pretty diversified, but his interests have one thing in common. There's always a bunch of money involved and he's supposed to be the one with the fat bankroll," she answered.

Stephen thought, wonderful, not only do I have to compete against a guy who has Anne's loyalty, but now I find out his reputation as a lover equals his prowess in finance.

Brandie Sue continued, "One time he came back to Mobile when a local savings and loan was in trouble. He not only got it back on track but he increased its profits so much that the chairman of the board's wife took off to Vegas with Taylor to celebrate, leaving her hubby and kids behind. Now that's a real show of appreciation." She paused to catch her breath and then asked innocently, "Do you think Anne would drop everything if Taylor helped her out of her mess?"

"What do you know about Anne's business situation?" Stephen asked.

"It's no secret. The whole town's abuzz--Livingston Enterprises is, or should I say, was a big deal. When Anne's grandfather handed it over to her, everybody thought it would fold overnight, but it didn't. Funny, though, how she lost control of the company just when its stock was selling like mad." Brandie Sue carefully watched Stephen's reaction.

Then she added, "Wouldn't it be something if Taylor rescued Anne's company just like he did that S&L? He'd be a hero in her eyes, wouldn't he?"

"Yeah, a real prince," Stephen answered, frowning at the thought of Anne being in Taylor's debt. If her gratitude ever turned to affection, Stephen knew she would be lost to him forever.

"Oh, yes, Taylor's some kind of guy--has a great sense of timing, too," Brandie Sue said, winking flirtatiously.

Stephen abruptly folded his napkin and placed it on the table. "Excuse me, I need some air," he said, leaving Brandie Sue in the company of the van Courts who'd returned to the table after visiting with other friends in the gallery.

Inhaling the crisp night air, Stephen turned when he heard Anne call his name and ask, "What are you doing out here by yourself?"

"Clearing my head," he replied, unwilling to admit the truth that he couldn't stand listening to one more word from Brandie Sue about Anne and Taylor.

"I'm surprised. I thought you were enjoying your little table treat," Anne said accusingly.

"What are you talking about?"

"You men are all alike. A pretty face, big eyes, and a little giggle or two and you're goners. Why, if you'd leaned any closer to her, you would've been in her lap. You seemed so cozy. That's why I left," she confessed.

"You've got to be kidding, Anne. You left me stranded. I looked up to say something to you, and you were gone. So, tell me, what was I supposed to do? Leave Brandie Sue by herself while I tracked you down?"

"No, of course not. You did the right thing, but did you have to enjoy your babysitting duty so much?" She hated that she sounded jealous and wondered why she felt that way.

She reminded herself that Stephen was just a business acquaintance, a man who would soon return to his home office and the life he'd left behind. Then she recalled the way his arms had felt around her and how much she'd relished his deep kisses.

Stephen, still bothered by Brandie Sue's comments about Anne and Scott and Anne and Taylor, said, "Talking about childcare, did you have fun with your med student?"

She retorted quickly, "For your information, Scott's a physician and he doesn't need anyone to take care of him."

"Oh really," he answered. "Where is the dashing young doctor?"

"Answering a page, so I told him I'd see him back at the table."

Stephen laughed and teased, "Bet he's on the line with his mother. It's probably past his curfew. How old is that guy anyway?"

"Stephen! As far as Scott's age, he's a lot more experienced and mature than his looks might lead you to think."

"Well, I don't know what to think. I thought I was your escort for tonight. I didn't know that we'd be seated with other people for the entire evening."

"That's what people do at dinner parties, Stephen. That way couples who already know everything about each other don't spend hours chatting with the people they know like the back of their hand. It makes for a more interesting time," she explained patiently.

Stephen folded his arms across his chest and grinned, "Well, that's dandy for old married types, but it doesn't seem quite fair to split up a couple that's just getting to know one another."

"Oh, so now we're a couple?" she asked teasingly.

"You tell me," he answered, smiling broadly as he took Anne into his arms and breathed gently into her left ear. Brushing her hair away with his lips, he placed a row of feathery kisses along the back of her neck. He felt her body respond to his.

"Anne, I don't know what kind of a relationship we have, but I do know that you're driving me crazy," he admitted. He wanted to tell her exactly what her nearness was doing to him, instead, he drew her closer to him and let his body show her what was on his mind.

Protected by the shadows of oleanders and hawthorns, their bodies moved to the rhythm of love, transporting them heavenward as each kiss became more electrifying the closer they touched.

"Pardon me, sir, ma'am. Dessert's now being served in the main dining room," an embarrassed waiter said and quickly retreated inside.

Stephen reluctantly released Anne, saying, "I'd rather take mine out here under the stars. What about you, Miss Livingston? What's your pleasure?"

"I think we should rejoin the others or..."

"Or what? People might talk. Is that it?" he asked.

"No, not really," she replied but still she didn't want tales spread about her and her handsome date from back East. If that news got out, she'd have more explaining to do. Her hands were already full--not only did she have to smooth things over with Taylor, she also needed to see her grandfather. She wanted him to hear the company news from her and her alone.

"Let's go inside now," she said, smoothing her skirt and moistening her lips.

Stephen placed his arm around her waist and guided her back inside the main room. He paused when out of the corner of his eye, he caught a glimpse of a shadowy figure holding court at the bar in the Oak Salon. "Damn that Hamilton," he mumbled under his breath. That's when he decided to put on a show of his own.

He led Anne back to their hosts' table and held her chair to seat her comfortably. Then, for all to see, especially the preening jerk at the bar, he took her hand and raised it to his lips. Kissing her slowly, he looked into her eyes and said, "Thank you for the tour of the gardens. The beauty of the flowers pales in comparison to yours, my love."

Brandie Sue fumed, Scott sulked, and Mr. van Court beamed as he asked, "Anne, has Bull met this young man?" Not receiving an immediate response, he added, "No? Well then, I suggest he do so and pretty soon." Turning to his wife, he asked, "Don't you think so, dear?"

"Oh, yes, I think it's about time," Mrs. van Court said as she smiled sweetly at Anne who blushed crimson.

Proud of his open declaration, Stephen rejoiced privately as he watched Taylor stalk outside. Stephen wasn't about to let anyone interfere with his pursuit of Anne. He marveled at the strength of the attraction he felt for her--never before had he thought about actually courting someone. But now he knew he'd found the woman of his dreams and he wasn't about to let her go.

Although tempted to put his life on hold, he decided that first he should prove his worth to Anne, as well as to her family and friends. How he would do it he wasn't quite sure, but he knew his effort would be rewarded a million times over. Holding Anne as tightly as he had and tasting her divine kisses had opened his eyes and his heart. Whatever it took, he was willing to give his all. Anne Livingston would soon be his. That was his mission and he was ready for the task.

"Sir? Are you finished?" inquired a waiter who appeared behind Stephen.

"Oh yes, I'm sorry," Stephen replied. "I was thinking about something."

"Anyone care for some creme liqueur?" Mr. van Court asked, looking at Anne and Stephen.

"Thank you, sir, but we need to start our drive back to town," she answered, smiling at the van Courts as she reached for her gloves and evening bag. The delicate beads of her dress reflected the warm glow of the flickering candles in the silver candelabra as she rose from the chair Stephen held for her.

Expressing their appreciation for a wonderful dinner, Anne and Stephen bid the van Courts and the other guests goodnight and started to walk away.

"Hold on, Stephen," Mr. van Court called. "If you're plan-ning on staying in town a while, I'd be honored if you and Anne would be my guests at my society's Mardi Gras ball."

Flattered but knowing he had to decline the invitation, Stephen said, "Thank you, sir, but I'm due back at work. Tomorrow's my last day here, unfortunately."

As much as he wanted to stay, Stephen knew his time in the Mobile area was drawing to a close. He was also well aware of his compelling desire to be near Anne. Wishing he could get her to relocate up North where executive positions were more plentiful, he wondered what it would take.

"Well, son, I'm sorry to hear that you're leaving us, I was hoping we might see a lot more of you."

Mrs. van Court watched Anne's face drain of color. Giving her a hug, she whispered, "Don't fret, he'll be back, sweetie, you'll see." To Stephen, she said, "You are coming back, aren't you?"

"Yes, ma'am, that's a promise," he swore as he tried to soften the sadness he saw in Anne's eyes. "I will definitely be back, and soon."

Brandie Sue joined the conversation by saying, "Stephen, I've a great idea. Since you can't make the ball, why don't you come downtown tomorrow night? Anne probably didn't tell you, but my society's parading and I'm going to be on one of the floats. Maybe if I see you, I'll throw more than a kiss your way."

"Give it a rest," Scott whispered to Brandie Sue. "He's not interested in you."

"We'll see about that," she countered. "Especially if I fix things so Taylor'll think Anne's hot for him. Bet you a stethoscope he'll have her tied up in mink and chains before you can say, 'Nurse.' That'll leave Stephen looking for comfort, and I'm ready and willing to take care of his every need."

"Don't get involved, Brandie Sue. Taylor doesn't like playing games. We all, and especially you, know that," Scott warned.

"Oh, pooh. You're no fun, Scott," she whined, watching Stephen lead Anne into the night.

On their way to the car, Anne regaled Stephen with tales of parade antics and merry maskers. "So what do you think? Do you want to brave the crowd?"

"Sure, it's a date, if I can get a later flight," he answered as they strolled hand and hand. Laughing, he said, "Now tell me again about those sugar beads."

CHAPTER 8

"This looks promising--no flats, no broken windows. Maybe our worries are over," Stephen said as he kicked at the tires of his car and checked under the hood.

Anne watched him carefully examine the tailpipe for tampering and said, "I think our imaginations got the best of us. That driver was probably caught in a bind and in a hurry with absolutely no intention of harming us." She waited for Stephen to respond and when he didn't, she added, "It makes more sense for us to forget the whole situation and move on, don't you agree?"

Although he answered, "Sure," not wanting to argue the point, he very warily opened her door and checked under the front seat for snakes, firecrackers, or bombs, just in case.

"Now are you satisfied?" she asked, fidgeting beside the car. "After all, the valet drove here safely from the parking lot."

Stephen grinned sheepishly, bowed from the waist, and said, "Yes, ma'am, the coast seems clear so let's go." He waited until she was comfortably seated and then walked to his side of the car. Before getting in, he casually glanced over his shoulder and seeing no sign of an intruder, he slid behind the wheel and started the engine.

Anne shook her head at his precautionary moves that he didn't know she'd observed.

As he drove toward the main road, he said, "Thank you for tonight. The van Courts were more than kind, they're an exceptional couple."

"I could tell they liked you, too, but then, you are a charmer."

"What?"

"You heard me, Stephen Richards. I watched your performance with Brandie Sue."

"Are you making something of nothing?" He shook his head in mock disgust.

She laughed lightly, her spirit free of cares, at least for the moment, but then her eyes sparked fire and ice. "Wait a minute, Stephen, you turned right out of the drive back there. We're headed the wrong way."

"Matter of opinion," he replied. "Didn't you tell me a beach paradise was close by?"

"Well, yes, but most people see it during the day, not in the middle of the night."

"It's not that dark--look at all the stars. The sky's filled with them. Can you name the constellations?"

"A few," she answered, thinking how much she'd always enjoyed stargazing. Then she shyly studied him from underneath her fringed eyelashes, wondering whether he was a shooting star or a rocket.

Blushing at her thoughts, she turned her head to look out the window as they passed through the small towns of Magnolia Springs and Foley. Not surprised that most of the coastal style homes set beside the road were dark inside, she imagined that the residents had turned in hours ago for a peaceful night's rest. She lowered her window to enjoy the soft, gentle breeze that seemed to buoy them down Highway 98 toward the Gulf.

"Have you driven this way before?" she asked.

"Never, this is my maiden voyage," he answered, keeping his eyes keenly focused on the narrow road that wound through open fields and pecan groves.

"You certainly seem to know where you're going and without asking for any directions."

"Maybe I did my homework."

"Right, and now you expect an A."

"Nope, better than that. I'm going for an A+ summa cum laude," he replied half-teasing.

She laughed with him, thoroughly enjoying their midnight drive. Then she thought about his leaving and her mood changed. "Do you really have to go tomorrow?"

"I wish I could stay, but I can't. Now if I were independently wealthy, I wouldn't have to worry about paying for food and rent."

"Alimony and child support, too?" she asked, trying not to sound either too obvious or too nosy.

He cast Anne a sideways glance, pleased that she seemed curious about his personal life. "I have neither an ex-wife wanting me to fund a new ball gown nor any children needing shoes for school. What you see is what you get. Just me, that's all."

"Oh, I see," she said, adding, "I wasn't prying but I thought I should know more, you know, since we're, uh, we're..." She struggled for the right words.

"Spending time together?"

"Yes, that's it," she answered.

"Does that mean you think of me as more than a business associate?"

"Hold it right there." Bristling, she sat up straight and pointed an accusatory finger at him. "You are not my associate. In fact, technically, what you are is an accessory to a terrible deed, an aider, an abettor, or worse. I probably shouldn't be with you now but since I am, I'm putting you on notice that I'm on my guard."

He listened patiently as she continued to lay down the law, but when she paused to catch her breath, he steadied the steering wheel with his left hand and reached for her still pointing finger with his right.

"What are you doing?" she asked, feeling the car slow to a crawl and then stop off the shoulder of the road.

Without offering any explanation, Stephen gently tugged on her finger, raised it to his mouth, and teased it with the tip of his tongue. When he met no resistance, he increased his pressure slightly.

Chills ran through Anne's body as somewhere off in the distance a bell tolled once. "One a.m., Stephen. It's a new day."

"Forget the time," he said, continuing to blaze a trail with his tongue from her fingertips to her wrist.

"Time--what's that?" she said with a sigh that came from deep inside her. She closed her eyes and dreamed of Stephen kissing her, touching her, loving her.

"Ooh," she said, when she felt a line of fire race through her. "I'm not dreaming, am I?" she said, her voice quivering almost as much as her thighs when she realized that Stephen's fingers searched underneath her skirt for the heart of her burning desire. Feeling torn between sensibility and sensuality, she debated what to do. The inner pull of her womanhood won. She slipped off her panty-hose and welcomed Stephen's caresses.

He tenderly stroked her baby-soft skin as he moved his hands between her legs. Inch by inch and higher and higher, he touched her here, he loved her there. When he felt the lace trim of her silk panties, he nudged the garment aside and pushed inside ever so slowly. There his fingers met the honey of her sweetness.

"Uh, oh," Anne moaned with lusty innocence.

"Do you want me to stop?" he asked, filled with desire for her and wanting to show her how he felt.

"I think you'd better," she said, glancing frantically in the side-view mirror.

"Must I?"

"Lights, Stephen, look at the flashing lights behind us," she gasped.

"Damn," he said, thinking, why now?

She hurriedly rearranged her skirt and reached for her compact to touch up her makeup. When she lowered the mirror behind the sun visor, she shook her head and said, "Saved in the knick of time by one of Alabama's finest. It's a cop."

Sweating from the heat of the moment and the thick night air, Stephen mopped his forehead and waited for the state trooper to approach his side of the car. He watched the beam from the officer's flashlight dance over the license plate on the rear bumper and then move from the back of the car to the center of his face.

Shading his eyes from the blinding light, he asked, "What is it, sir? I don't believe I did anything wrong."

"Are you arguing with me, mister?" the scowling officer asked to which Stephen wisely replied, "No, sir."

Anne tried to appear calm and remained silent.

"May I see your drivers' license?"

Stephen handed it over and waited as the officer read it.

He flicked his fingers against the license and said, "What is this? Rhode Island? Hmm, you're a long way from home."

"I'm here on business," Stephen answered curtly.

"I see. Where's your car registration?" He moved his head close in toward Stephen's and stared at him long and hard.

Feeling more uncomfortable by the moment, Stephen coughed nervously and replied, "This isn't my car--it's a rental, the papers are probably in the glove compartment." He looked at Anne pleadingly and asked, "Would you check? Please?"

She dug them out and passed them to Stephen who handed them over.

The surly trooper frowned as he examined the paperwork. Narrowing his eyes at the couple, he pointed the beam of his flashlight toward their feet. Slowly he moved the light upwards, but then quick as a fox, he shot the beam back down at Anne's barefeet. He snickered, turned the light off, and stepped away from the car.

Stephen breathed easier and Anne kicked at her panty-hose, hoping the officer hadn't seen them crumpled on the floor. She bent over to retrieve one of her shoes but stopped when the officer's light suddenly flashed through the open window on her side of the car.

He leered toward her and said, "Had a big night out, I see. Pretty fancy dress, missy, looks real nice."

Stephen fumed silently for a moment and then, annoyed with the man and his attitude, asked, "Sir, is that all?"

The trooper ignored Stephen's question as he turned his flashlight beam on Anne's face. "You all right, ma'am?"

"Yes, officer, I'm fine. Thank you for your concern," she replied, hoping he'd leave.

"Your accent tells me you're one of ours. From around here?"

"I live and work in Mobile, but I wanted to show Stephen, uh, I mean, Mr. Richards, my family's beach cottage at Fort Morgan. That's where we're going," she stammered.

Thinking, this is news, Stephen whistled and smiled.

"Something funny, Mr. Richards?" the officer asked.

"That does it," Stephen retorted, feeling a surge in his blood pressure. "Tell me what law I broke."

Locking eyes with Stephen, the officer said, "Well, since your papers seem to be in order, I'm going to let you go although someone radioed in a description of a stolen car that matches the one you're driving."

"What?" Stephen and Anne asked in unison.

"That's right. The caller also indicated a potential abduction might be in progress but since the lady here seems, ah,..." He paused and then added with a smutty grin, "Seems satisfied with her situation, you're free to leave. Remember though, I'll be watching you on down the road." The trooper shot Stephen one last menacing look and then he returned to his squad car.

Anne closed her eyes and sighed in relief, saying, "Oh my goodness, this evening has been full of surprises."

"It's not over yet," Stephen said as he watched her eyes flash open and seem to sparkle. "The ride's just started," he added, firing the ignition and pulling back onto the highway. Although tempted to test the engine's horsepower, he didn't dare as the trooper's words of warning echoed in his ears. Stephen looked in the rear-view mirror and cursed under his breath.

"What is it? Is he behind us?" Anne asked.

"On our tail, I'm afraid." Driving the speed limit, he thought, please, no tickets, no jail, not tonight. A soft, sandy beach was much more to his liking.

"Why'd she lie to me about tonight? Where is she now?" Taylor growled to the stark walls of his penthouse as he stormed from one room to another. "If she thinks she can take off with that chump and leave me to cool my heels, she's got somethin' else comin'."

Ripping off his tie and loosening his shirt collar that was a size too small, he threw his cordless phone against the wall. "Damn phone's no use if the bitch isn't there to answer," he raved as he stalked to his bar.

He downed a double shot of whiskey and said, "Fastest damn recovery I've ever seen. She's an actress, pulled off an academy award-winnin' performance--poor Anne's goin' to see dear ol' granddad. What a crock--by damn, she's almost as good a user as I am. Well, if she thinks she can best ol' Taylor, she's in for a surprise. Yessiree, I've got a job for her, one she won't forget."

Taylor allowed his anger to rage, seeming to gain positive strength from his outbursts. He knew that being out of sorts almost always set the stage for some of his better schemes-- he liked to use his time wisely. He thought about his recently acquired holdings and said, "The paper mills aren't producin' so I gotta find a sap to take them off my hands, but my Livingston deal's gonna make me a bundle. Yep, all it needed was my touch and a few dirty bucks. Too bad for little Anne, but such a suga' plum for Taylor." He laughed so hard that the roll of fat around his middle shook.

He smiled to himself, knowing that he'd been in the right place at the right time, ready to silently step in and soothe the hidden woes of Livingston Enterprises. So what that fabrication played a large role in the investor scare he'd concocted? So what he'd promoted the hoax using an assumed identity? "Big damn deal," he scoffed.

Taylor had learned early on that perceived fear promoted an even greater fear, especially where nervous investors were concerned. He'd practiced the art of setting takeovers in motion and then hiring clueless minions to handle the paperwork for his dummy corporations that he coded by initials, instead of by name. "Let's hear it for 'TMK'--The Master King," he shouted. "Bring me my crown!"

He laughed almost hysterically as he thought of his kingdom, the many corporations he'd manipulated at one time or another. Adding Anne's operation was his latest coup, one that he believed promised an even greater reward-- the former president herself. Hell, he thought, I've already removed her from the boardroom, now it's time for her to assume her proper place in my bedroom.

Thinking about the opportunity gladdened his spirit and another generous shot of whiskey added to his celebratory mood. He felt superior to the likes of Stephen Richards, fully believing that he was the better man. After all, he reported to no one, but men like Stephen had to face a boss. "The smug S.O.B.'s just a loser puppet who doesn't even know who's pullin' his strings," Taylor crowed as he staggered back to his bar.

"How about a squeeze around the neck, Stevie? Yes indeed, you deserve it. Anyway, who asked you to stick around?"

Taylor studied his empty glass and proclaimed, "If that clown thinks Taylor Hamilton's goin' let him sniff around his intended, well, he's askin' to learn a real hard lesson and I'm ready to knock his head against the blackboard."

He stripped off his clothes and paraded naked in front of a mirrored door. Attempting to flex his triceps that merely hung loose with flab, he said, "As for you, Annie doll, so you wanna play a little game with me. That's good, 'cause I love pursuit when it turns to a chase."

Struggling into his robe, he thought, idiot laundry shrunk the damn thing. Then his mind flashed again to Anne. He pictured her sweet curves that he planned to have surgically enhanced and said, "So she thinks makin' me jealous will spice up our relationship. Well then, she'd best get ready for cayenne 'cause I'm holdin' the shaker."

Taylor tried Anne's telephone number another time and let it ring until her answering machine picked up. As her greeting played, he mouthed into the receiver, "Instead of wastin' your diminishin' dollars on gourmet cat food, you oughtta make that bag of fleas earn its keep. Teach it somethin' valuable, like pickin' up your damn phone. I'd rather talk to that fur ball than your stinkin' machine. Yeah, yeah...I'll leave a message at the beep..."

He fixed another drink, clicked on his computer, and pulled up his "Babe File." Skimming through the "B" section list of names, telephones numbers, and ratings, he mused,

maybe there's somethin' to first initials and personal attri-
butes--Brandie Sue's definitely "B-team" but Anne's an "A"
or at least she will be after I redesign her. Sneering, he
dialed Brandie Sue's number.

"Hello?" Brandie Sue said drowsily, answering her phone
on its tenth ring.

"Why, hi there, sleepyhead darlin'. Tell me I didn't disturb
your beauty rest."

"Who is this?"

"Now you've done it, Brandie Sue. You've gone and hurt
your ol' pal Taylor's feelin's."

Silent for a few minutes, she put her finger on the discon-
nect button and almost pressed it.

"Brandie Sue, baby face, are you there? Now I know I was
a real bad boy the last time I saw you and for that I apologize.
So how about hearin' me out, sweet eyes? Please?"

"I hate you, Taylor Hamilton!" Brandie Sue shouted into
the phone. "You're nothing to me anymore, so why should
I waste my time listening to you? I should've had you ar-
rested for what you took from me."

"Ooh, baby, I said I'd been a bad boy and I'm sorry. I'm
different now, all because of you."

"What?" she asked, her voice riddled with disbelief.

"That's right, rose petal. You taught me a lot and now I'm
a changed man. For that, I have you to thank--and that's
why I'm callin' you. Seein' you tonight over at Point Clear
made me remember the good ol' days of you and me. I've
really missed bein' with you, darlin'."

"You're crazy, Taylor. You haven't called me for years, so
why now? What do you want?"

"Just to show you I'm sorry," he said, trying to sound
sincere.

"Sorry? Sorry for leaving me behind with a bad reputation
or sorry for all your lies?"

Taylor could see her brown eyes flashing as she tried to
lay him low. "Now, honey pie," he cooed.

"Heavens, Taylor! You swore you loved me and that you'd
never leave, but guess what? After you got what you wanted,

you split, leaving me to sweat out the pregnancy tests all by myself."

"I'm sorry, suga' lips. I did you wrong and for that I'm so, so ashamed of myself. I guess I just needed some time to grow up," he said, becoming bored with the conversation. He wondered how many more apologies he'd have to make before he could get what he needed out of her. He'd done it before but this time the stakes were higher than the nights of fun she'd given him in the back waters of Bon Secour Bay.

He took a deep breath and started his onslaught anew. "Remember all our good times, angel face. Like when you said that my daddy's boat was better than a waterbed. Don't tell me you've forgotten the way we made waves! Didn't you call me 'Hurricane Taylor'--your love machine?"

Brandie Sue tapped her polished fingernails on the phone and said, "Oh yes, I remember that and more. Especially when you burned up the road to Tuscaloosa and left me scared and alone at Lake Forest. For God's sake, Taylor, you were my first love, you, you..."

"Let me make it up to you, lil' darlin'. You've always had a special place in my heart." Taylor felt his patience clock ticking and knew his boredom alarm was about to ring.

"Do you still care about me?" she asked, her tone of voice softening.

Taylor grinned, thinking, bingo, gotcha darlin'. Leaning back in his chair, he whispered like a saint, "I promise you can trust ol' Taylor."

Brandie Sue smiled. "I'm not betting on that anymore, Taylor Hamilton. Anyway, I'm smarter now. Being with you taught me more than learning to count the days between my periods."

"What?" he asked, surprised by her candor.

Drawing "X's and O's" on a notepad, she said, "It's this way. You and I can call things even if you help me get something I want."

"You want to use me?" he asked incredulously.

"That's right, Taylor. It's time for us to bury the past and chart new territory."

Intrigued, Taylor said, "That's my girl. Hold that thought while I get somethin' to drink." Returning to the phone with a bottle of Southern Comfort in his hand, he sipped and listened as Brandie Sue outlined her plan to push Anne off on him so she'd have a clear shot at Stephen. "Let me be sure I have this straight, you're saying that you'll forgive me if I promise to sleep with another woman?"

"Yes, that's it, but Stephen must think 'Little Miss Perfect' Anne Livingston ran to your bed."

Seeing that picture, he bellowed, "Hot damn, Brandie Sue! I love you, cupcake. This merger deserves a toast, so how about I come on over?"

"Okay, when?"

"Now."

"Now?" she asked. "I'm not sure that's a very good idea, you know, you and me alone."

Taylor snarled to himself, this woman's still as dumb as dirt if she thinks I have a thing for her. To Brandie Sue he said as genuinely as he could fake it, "You can believe in me, angel eyes. I just want us to kiss and make up, nothin' else, I promise."

"Well then, I guess it's all right. But Taylor, I'm warning you. If you as much as lay one hand on me, I'm calling the law."

"Don't worry, my butterfly beauty. I'll behave," he answered smuggly. "You still live with your parents in Spring Hill?"

"Yes and no. I'm housesitting for them while they're in Colorado."

"Okay, then. I'll see you in about an hour."

As Brandie Sue prepared for Taylor's visit, she dusted off two silver wine chalices and said, "My prayer's been answered. Life on the Eastern seaboard with a handsome man is just what I need." Puckering her lips, she studied her reflection in the goblets and said, "A one-way ticket to Connecticut or was it Rhode Island? Who cares? Stephen's a hunk, acts rich, and he's oh, so sexy."

Following Anne's directions, Stephen turned off the main highway at Gulf Shores and started the drive down the Fort Morgan Road. They passed some older settlements that faced Bon Secour Bay where generations had spent decades fishing and oystering.

"Quaint village," Stephen said, admiring a row of weathered cottages set at the water's edge. "And look over there, an elephant could hide in that," he added, pointing at some huge, moss-draped live oaks that served as a natural barricade.

"No kidding," Anne said, delighting in the excitement she saw in Stephen's eyes. "In fact, the locals say that pirates stashed their plunder all around here. Oyster Bay has quite a colorful reputation."

He slowed the car, causing Anne to suggest, "Let's tour the area tomorrow--it's too late now."

"Nope, I can't wait to start our treasure hunt," he answered, stopping the car between a stand of tall pines alongside the road that separated Bon Secour Bay on the right from the Gulf beaches on the left.

Anne opened her eyes wide. Although she had a pretty good idea of his intent, she asked anyway, "Why are we really stopping here?"

"I want to get my bearings before we go much farther. Seems like we're running out of civilization or is that only my imagination?" He turned off the ignition, got out, and walked to Anne's side of the car. "Let's see what's out here, I'll go first," he said, as he opened her door and helped her step down. With much bravado, he bellowed, "Watch out pirates, here I come."

Laughing at his antics, she followed closely behind as he cleared a path through the low brush.

"Come here, Anne, this way," he called.

She stepped through the tall grasses and reached for his hand. Suddenly she felt the earth give way under her feet as she slipped in the marshy soil.

Coming to her rescue, Stephen caught her as she fell toward him. He pulled her closer and held her as though she was made of fine china. Unable to resist her beauty, he kissed her forehead and then her eyes.

His breath warmed the delicate skin of her eyelids as he traced their shape with the tip of his tongue. Lightly caressing the corners of her eyes, he tasted and teased first one side and then the other. He then slowly moved lower. His lips barely brushed against hers, making her cry out for more.

"You're beautiful, but you already know that," he whispered as he touched the rising fullness of one of her breasts and stroked a hard nipple that strained to be released from its enclosure of satin. Unable to rein in his desire, he sought her willing lips that parted without hesitation as his tongue met hers.

Anne felt her whole being yield to Stephen's heart-stopping kiss. Filled with burning sensations so strong that she thought she might explode in a burst of flames, she struggled to catch her breath. When she tried to speak, the only words she could form were "More, more."

He complied with her request, quieting the sounds of the night with touches and kisses so intense that Anne believed she was about to lose all touch with reality. Never had she felt so aroused, so reckless. Without a thought as to propriety or privacy, she wondered if Stephen would transport her above the stars. She wanted her body to fly, to soar.

The breeze from the water lifted her long hair, allowing Stephen to feel its silkiness as he carefully lowered her to a bed of pine straw that softened the forest floor. "Anne, I want you and I want you now," he pleaded, devouring her with his eyes and his kisses.

"I want you, too," she moaned as she felt his strong hands press between her burning thighs. "Yes, oh yes, now," she cried.

Cradling her in his arms, he began to unzip her dress. Hoarsely, he whispered, "Undress me," as he guided her hands to his waist.

Without hesitation, she unfastened first his belt and then his zipper. She shivered with excitement when she felt him respond to her touch as her hand tentatively moved to the top of his thighs.

Suddenly a piercing wail disrupted their closeness, causing Stephen to curse.

Sitting up, Anne looked at Stephen apologetically. "Oh, I'm sorry, that's my pager. I dropped it in my purse before we left town."

"Are you expecting a call at 2 a.m.?"

"No, of course not. But I worry that my grandfather might need me, so I always keep a communication line open." Not wanting to spoil the moment, she blocked out her nagging fear that the page she'd missed signaled that more anxiety was headed her way.

Kissing the tip of her nose, Stephen said, "You're going to be the death of me, Anne Livingston. Are you carrying any other bells, whistles, or alarms? If so, tell me now so I can order a pacemaker."

They looked at each other and burst into laughter. Sharing a carpet of pine needles in the middle of nowhere, they took turns fastening each other's clothing that moments before they'd so intently tried to discard.

"Our night's not over yet, you little sea sprite. You're very elusive, but I'm going to hear your siren's song before the break of day." He kissed her again and whispered, "That's a promise I intend to keep."

CHAPTER 9

Anne stretched her arms above her head and cautiously opened one eye. Toward Pensacola, the sun was just beginning to rise, flooding her bedroom with brilliant light. The early morning glare jolted her memory, causing her to gasp, "Oh, no, I'm naked! What have I done?"

She pulled her pink cotton sheets tightly around her neck and squeezed her eyes shut. "I can't believe I did this--I can't believe I did this," she sighed repeatedly, but then she opened her eyes wide and surveyed the damage. A trail of clothing, hers and his, littered the carpeting from the front door to the bedroom of her tiny cottage by the sea.

"Oh, dear God, it's really true. We made love all night long and now I'm here alone. He's gone," she sobbed into her pillow. Wishing the down feathers would swallow her whole, she shuddered as memories of the night before came clearly into focus.

She and Stephen had stopped at the public boat ramp by the Bay where she'd only meant to show him the sparkling water, not the passion he'd aroused in her.

Thinking, thank heavens no one drove by, she remembered how they'd caressed, trading a kiss for each star they could name and two for those they couldn't. They'd totally lost themselves in the deep indigo sky and had become entranced by the movement of the waves and the motion of their bodies that meshed together into one sweet form.

She trembled at the memory of Stephen's kisses that had penetrated her soul. He'd asked if she was sure she wanted to be with him that way and she'd answered, "Yes, oh yes." She recalled turning her face toward his hungry lips and embracing him passionately.

Sitting up in bed, she shivered with the remembered sensation. "The kiss, the damn kiss, that's what started it," she said, shaking her head to ward off the memory of what they'd done next that rushed through her mind.

He'd carried her back to his car, kissed her deeply, and placed his hand lovingly over her heart. She could still hear him say, "You won't regret this, sweetheart, I promise."

"Promises, promises," she wailed, muffling her cries with her sheets. "I should've made him drive straight into the Bay, anywhere but here." Filled with remorse, she sank into her mattress as memories of the last few miles of their drive became real once again.

She'd rested her head against his broad shoulder as he'd placed his right hand between her thighs. Stroking her passionately, he'd hastened their drive on down the beach road as she'd given him directions to her family's cottage.

The words she'd spoken then haunted her now. "Turn left by the Flag Shop and head straight for the beach, then take a right."

She worried that she'd seemed too anxious and she wished that she hadn't been so ready, but her body had overpowered her intellect. "This is so unlike me," she said, knowing that she rarely dated and when she did, she rationed her kisses like stock market tips. "I couldn't help myself, I honestly couldn't," she cried, remembering the way her entire being had responded to his every move and oh, he'd moved so divinely.

Trembling with the memory of Stephen kissing almost every inch of her body, she relived the moment when he'd given her throbbing center life. Yes, she had to admit that was when she'd thrown caution the way of the shifting sands--and as a result, she'd spent the most amazing night of her life.

"Oh, come on," she chided herself. "If the night was so great, then why am I here by myself?" She moaned with shame as she held her head in her hands. Then she remembered exactly what had made the night so incredible, so unforgettable.

Crazed with shared desire, they'd ripped off their clothes, piece by piece, until they'd both stood naked in the living room, transforming it into their own private playroom.

"How could I?" she wailed, remembering she'd tossed her bra and panties in the exact spot where her parents had decorated Christmas trees for their family holidays at the beach. Anne felt salty tears running down her cheeks. "I'm such a fool," she cried. Then Stephen's image flooded her mind, stopping her tears.

He'd become so hard when she'd taken his maleness into her mouth and he'd excited her beyond sanity when he'd found her rising mound and had tasted her milky honey. She remembered screaming with sheer passion at the pleasure he'd given her with his lips, his tongue, his hands.

She caught a glimpse of herself in the mirror on the dresser by her antique brass bed. Weeping loudly, she cried, "I can't believe I did this in the very bed my grandparents slept in. Oh, no, what came over me? I don't make love unless I am in love."

Stunned by her own admission, she stared straight ahead and gasped, "Oh dear God, I've fallen in love with a Yankee!"

Two gulls flew by her window, cooing lovingly as they caught a wind current and glided by, a perfect pair. Her mind flashed to another perfect match--her body entwined with Stephen's. He'd waited patiently for her to peak, delaying his own release until she'd fallen over the edge, over and over again. She could still feel his constant, rhythmic stroking, in and out, in and out.

"Ooh," she sighed, savoring the memory. He'd made her feel as though she was the most special woman in the world. The hours had passed unnoticed as they couldn't get enough of each other. In her mind, it had been sheer heaven complete with skyrockets bursting over the lighthouse at the end of the island.

She finger-combed her hair and reached for a tissue to wipe away her tears. She closed her eyes and shook her head at reality, unable to ignore the grains of sand lodged between her rumpled sheets that clearly told the story of a night of passion and love.

She picked up some of the sugary sand and remembered dashing outside with Stephen for a quick dip in the cool Gulf waters. After playing in the crashing surf, they'd found a dune covered with tall sea oats in front of her cottage. There he'd tenderly caressed her breasts, taking his time fondling and teasing her nipples until she'd thought she might die. And she'd loved him back so exquisitely that he'd screamed with his release. Their passion had become so intense that they'd sworn they'd set the dunes on fire.

"Oh, no, the neighbors!" Anne gasped. "If they heard me beg, 'Now, Stephen, now!' and if they heard him cry, 'Oh Anne, my darling, my darling,' they know I was out there with a man." Pulling the sheets up around her head, she curled into the fetal position and waited to die. She couldn't bear the thought of facing old family friends and having to ask them for a ride back to Mobile since Stephen had left her stranded without a way home.

Tortured by guilt, she thought she might simply become a beachcomber, but her contemplation of that career move ended when she heard a deep male voice ask, "Where's my little CEO?"

"Stephen! You're still here," she said, feeling her heart race madly. Torn between delight and despair, she debated whether she should run to his arms or run far, far away.

He didn't give her a chance to do either as he playfully leaped onto the bed, causing the slats to fall out in a loud crash. "Oops! Must have been the Bananas Foster we had for dessert," he laughed as he reached for her. "Come here, my little sea sprite. I'm not finished with you yet," he teased, discarding his pants with one quick motion.

He gathered her up closely in his strong arms. Feeling his dark, downy chest hairs rub against her breasts shifted Anne's senses into overdrive. Surging heat traveled her spinal cord and headed to her burning core. "Oh, oh, oh Stephen," she said throatily.

"What is it, princess?" he asked, but he didn't wait for an answer. He already knew what was on her mind because her thoughts echoed his own.

So what the bed was in danger of falling apart? So what they'd already destroyed one set of sheets? So what the cottage moved with every turn and touch of their bodies as they rose and fell together? So what the gulls and pelicans seemed to fly closer by for a better look?

For the next hour, Stephen and Anne didn't pay any attention to the world around them. In fact, had their private pleasure island been invaded, they would've said, "Go ahead, take what you want. Just close the door on your way out."

After repeatedly coming to one another, they finally rested, snuggling together in their broken bed. "You're amazing," Stephen said, holding her hand to his heart.

"No, you are," she replied, tracing the outline of his nose with her fingertips.

"You were right, you know," he whispered softly.

"About what?"

"Without a doubt, this is paradise. How could anyone ever leave this beautiful place?"

Sad at the mention of parting, she frowned, knowing that soon he would have to go--out of her life, probably forever.

"Why the sad face, little one?" he asked, not liking the change in her expression. Having seen her float a million miles off of the ground, he felt her unhappiness tear at his heart. "What are you thinking?"

"When I woke this morning and saw that you weren't here, I told myself that I shouldn't have expected you to stay. After all, there's no permanence to our relationship. I should accept it for what it is."

"And what is that?"

"Oh, you know. Hot shot comes to town, meets a woman, toys with her heart and soul, and then takes off, never to be seen again."

Offended, he asked huffily, "Are you describing me or someone else?"

"What do you mean?"

"That your words better fit that blowhard friend of yours. You know, Taylor Hamilton."

Feeling the need to defend Taylor, she lectured, "Now, really, Stephen, he's not so bad. He actually has a good heart. Otherwise, he wouldn't have offered to help me get my career back on track."

"I don't think you should trust him so blindly," Stephen warned. "There's something about him that doesn't sit right with me."

"You just don't understand Taylor, that's all," she countered. "He's not such a bad guy. At least he'd never abandon me, unlike someone else."

"What's that supposed to mean?"

"Who let me wake up by myself this morning? How do you think I felt when I reached over and found myself alone?"

Stephen took Anne's face in his hands and kissed her flushed cheek. "Maybe I was on a mission for my sea siren."

"You're nuts, Stephen, do you know that?"

"Oh, yes, I'm nuts about you," he replied, nibbling on her chin.

"So tell me about your mission."

Stephen reached for his pants and dug into the back pocket that was filled with sand. "Here, I found this for you," he said, gently placing a round object in her right hand.

"Oh, Stephen, it's beautiful. How did you know that the sand dollar means so much to me?" She felt tears well up in her eyes.

Stephen beamed, knowing he'd pleased her. "Do you remember when we first met in your office?"

"How could I forget the day I lost my family's business as well as my job?" she asked incredulously.

Continuing, Stephen said, "That's when I saw the sand dollar you carried in your suit pocket. It came from this beach, didn't it?"

"Do you know all my secrets?"

He smiled and winked at her.

"Pretty perceptive for a Yankee," she teased.

"I'll Yankee you, you little devil," he answered with a laugh as he reached for her hand and kissed her fingertips.

Sighing she said, "I wish you could stay."

"Me, too," he answered.

She glanced at the clock on her white wicker nightstand and thought, each tick means our time's about to end. "Where do we go from here?" she asked, gazing at him with a look loaded with fire but tempered by reality.

"One day at a time, my love," he answered, blowing her a kiss as he headed for the shower.

She knew that she'd entered into a relationship where no promises had been made, so no promises could be broken, except for one. Hadn't he assured her that she wouldn't have any regrets?

Sitting with her arms curled around her bare legs, she listened to Stephen whistling in the shower as though he hadn't a care in the world. She knew that within minutes, he would dress and head for the door.

Better get moving, she thought, wondering what to put on since her dress was beyond repair from her all-night love fest. She opened a trunk where she kept a few changes of seaworthy clothes. "These'll do," she said, shaking out a pair of jeans and a denim shirt.

Stephen, wearing only a towel and a boyish grin, stood by the door and watched her slip into the jeans that fit her like a second skin. Smiling his approval, he asked, "Can you find something in that trunk for me?"

She dug deeper and came up with some jeans and a tattered flannel shirt her brother had worn. "How about these?" she asked, pitching them toward Stephen.

Catching them but losing his towel in the process, he bowed his "thanks" and winked as he backed into the bathroom.

While he finished grooming in the master bath, Anne sponge-bathed in a small bathroom down the hallway. Although she knew she should cleanse herself thoroughly, for some reason she didn't--she wasn't ready to let go of the part of Stephen she still carried inside.

Slipping into a pair of battered topsiders, she turned her attention to her hair. She twisted it into a loose braid, foregoing either a comb or pins to hold it in place, a trick she'd learned from her Eastern classmates who'd teased her about her Southern use of barrettes and bows to tame her wild locks.

Hearing, "Hello, gorgeous," she turned and smiled. Then feeling hands cupping her behind, she asked, "Whatever are you doing now?"

"What does it feel like?" Stephen nibbled on her ear lobe and loosened her hair with a gentle pull of his pearly white teeth.

"I think you know," she answered, feeling her passion pulse spike. "But we don't have time, especially if you're serious about staying on schedule. It's time for us to go."

"What if I'm not ready?" He placed her hands against his warm and freshly shaven face.

As she stroked his cheeks, she said, "You have to go, a job's waiting for you. Besides, if you don't watch out, you might catch the 'loser virus' from me."

"Anne, Anne," he said sternly. "You're too hard on yourself. If you didn't hear me the first or even the second time I told you this, then please listen to me now." He held her at arm's length to better maintain eye contact and said, "You did nothing wrong. In fact, maybe if you hadn't been so successful with Livingston Enterprises, then the raiders would never have noticed the sudden growth in your profit sheet."

"You're sweet to absolve me of responsibility for my company's failure, but that's something I have to accept. Just like I have to accept the fact that we need to get on the road. Give me a second to check the windows, a storm may come up before I have a chance to get back over here."

He watched her flit from room to room, so careful, so protective of her fragile world. He figured that she'd probably approached her business life with the same dedication. Wondering what had gone wrong at Livingston Enterprises, he decided that he would uncover the true story behind the acquisition.

In retrospect, the bottom line seemed far too clean. Wishing that he'd conducted a more thorough background search on the deal, he hoped now wasn't too late. He believed he was on to something shady but he felt this was neither the time nor place to involve Anne, she'd already endured more than the most experienced could handle, so adding to her burden was out of the question.

"Ready?" she asked, breaking Stephen from his thoughts.

"If you insist," he answered, as he helped her lock the door. On the deck, he paused for a last look at the rolling tide and the puffy clouds above. "Paradise found," he said with a sigh as they walked hand in hand down the creaky steps, feeling united in their spoken love for the Gulf and their unspoken love for one another.

With Stephen behind the wheel, they reversed their drive from the night before. "This all looks so different in daylight," he commented, noticing that the majesty of the tall pines gave way to dazzling displays of wildflowers and wisteria all along the road.

"I guess so," she said, relieved that Stephen's thoughts had become tourist-like. She wasn't ready to discuss their intense lovemaking or the possible consequences.

Even though neither brought up the subject of their shared passion, both knew something wonderful had occurred and their lives would never be the same as a result of the precious time they'd spent together. Wherever they looked, they saw something that reminded them of the night before.

Instead of seeing flowering vines intertwined through the lush foliage, Anne saw herself with Stephen, linked together in a lover's knot. As for Stephen, he knew he should concentrate on the S-curves that loomed ahead, but instead all he could think about were Anne's shapely curves that had given him such divine pleasure.

He watched her, thinking of the personal tragedies of her life. Helpless to change the past, he hoped to make the future better for her. If only he could uncover misdoings in the transaction process, then he could work to get the whole deal cancelled. That way, she would regain her company and he would have at least her gratitude, if not her heart.

"You seem preoccupied," she said.

"I was just thinking about seeing Brandie Sue on a float," he teased. "Did you really mean what you said last night about hating to share me with her?"

"Don't flatter yourself," Anne replied, ignoring the words she knew she'd spoken.

"If the riders are masked, how will I know which one's Brandie Sue?" he asked impishly.

Feeling suddenly jealous, she retorted, "I'll tell you how. Just look for the fattest woman stuffed in the tightest costume, that'll be Brandie Sue."

"Meow!" Stephen responded playfully.

"Well, it's the truth. Anyway, the parade starts about 6:30."

"Does it end at your street?" he asked hopefully.

She smiled and answered, "Thank goodness, no. Too many people and too much mess for me."

"Like the Mardi Gras parades in New Orleans?" he asked.

"Oh, ours aren't that wild but thousands usually show up for the one tonight because of all the trinkets the maskers throw to the crowd. I think you'll have a good time."

"Are you asking me for another date?" he teased.

Bristling, she fumed, "Who me? Asking you out? I think not. After all, if you will remember, you were the one who sweet-talked the van Courts out of a dinner invitation and then you were the driver who took us the wrong direction so we had no choice other than to spend the night at the beach."

"And what a night and morning it was," Stephen replied, beaming at Anne.

Changing the subject to safer territory, she asked, "What about tonight? Ready to brave a crowd of 30,000 party animals?"

"Sure, if I can switch flights. How long does the parade last?"

"Why? Are you in a hurry to leave town?"

"No, that's not it," he answered. "I was just wondering about the logistics of all those people and the traffic jams."

"Likely story," she replied. "You probably have a hot date waiting in the wings?"

"Why the suspicious nature, bright eyes?" he asked, tossing her a million dollar smile.

"Let's just say that I've been down this road before." Her body language gave away the truth--she'd been hurt and she still carried the memory of her pain.

"You're wrong about me, Anne. I'm someone you can trust and someway, somehow I'm going to prove it to you." He nodded his head for emphasis, realizing he'd made yet another promise.

"Yeah, right," she replied unconvinced.

"You'll see," he said, as he headed their car toward Foley. Waiting for a stoplight to change and not caring who saw, he leaned over and kissed her softly. "One of these days, Anne Livingston, you're going to wake up and realize that all men are not the enemy. Some can actually be trusted." As the light changed to green, he added, "Present company included."

In silence, they passed row after row of shopping centers, antique stores, and banks and businesses that served as the commercial center for South Baldwin County. Coming to a crossroads, he asked, "Which way do I go from here?"

"I thought you were Mr. Highway Wizard," she answered with a laugh. "Last night you didn't need any directions."

"Well, that was then," he replied good-naturedly. "But I just saw an I-10 sign back there. Should I follow it?"

"Sure, if you're in a hurry to pack your briefs, uh, briefcase, I mean."

He smiled and made a quick left turn.

"Wait a minute," she said, pointing frantically to the highway they'd just left. "To get to the interstate, you should go the other way."

"This way looks more interesting so if it's all right with you, Ms. Time Management, I think we'll take the scenic route. End of discussion." Stephen was no longer in a kidding mood--the time for fun and games had ended. Now he was going for broke and every extra moment he spent with her counted.

"You're unbelievable, Stephen. How does your boss handle your independent streak?"

"No office talk, I'll get an earful of that soon enough. My boss'll see to that."

"What's he like?" she asked, having decided she'd better find out more about Stephen, especially in light of the night they'd just spent together.

"Who said she's a he?" Stephen answered.

"Do you mean to tell me that you, Mr. GQ, answer to a woman?" She shook her head in mock disbelief.

"Look, I'm totally liberated and I thought you were too, especially given the way you called the shots last night."

"Stephen!" she gasped, feeling her cheeks redden.

Smiling, he disregarded a turn that probably would've saved them several miles, opting instead for a road that wound along the Eastern Shore. Not bothered by much traffic, he dropped below the speed limit, savoring the spectacular view.

"Why didn't you tell me about all these great homes on the water?" he asked. "They're amazing."

"This is a pretty drive," she agreed, feeling comfortable and happy with Stephen. "My family used to spend Labor Days at a house nearby that I always loved. It's coming up soon, I'll tell you when to stop."

Stephen admired the homes that were almost hidden from the road by huge oleanders that reached for the sky. "Are we getting close? I don't want to miss your special place."

Pleased that he seemed to appreciate the area that held lots of pleasant memories for her, she explained the meaning behind the names of some of the beautiful estates they passed. Then seeing a handpainted sign, "Bay View," she clapped her hands, pointed wildly, and said, "It's still there. What do you think?"

Whistling under his breath, he said, "Your taste is impeccable."

The house and grounds fronted Mobile Bay, but getting there looked like a challenge. Bordered on both sides by dozens of massive azalea bushes in full bloom, a long shell-covered drive snaked its way toward the house that was surrounded by acres of bermuda grass. "It'd take a week to cut all of that," he said, surveying the lush, manicured lawn.

Laughing, she said, "I'm sure they have a gardener."

"They need at least three," he replied, turning for a better view of the two-story plantation-style home that had a porch on three sides. "What a view," he marveled. "The sunrises and sunsets have got to be incredible."

"They are," she said with a sigh. "I really love this place."

"And I love you." Stephen caught his breath when he realized the magnitude of the words he'd just uttered barely above a whisper.

"Excuse me?" she asked.

"I just agreed that it's a lovely sight," he said. "Would you like to live there?"

"Oh yes, that's been one of my dreams for a long time," she said wistfully.

"I hope all your dreams come true," he said, reaching for her hand and making a secret wish of his own.

CHAPTER 10

"Where is he?" Anne asked as she looked up and down the sidewalk that overflowed with light-spirited revelers. She'd told Stephen to meet her at 5:30 on the parade route at the corner of Government and Conception Streets, but he was nowhere in sight.

Feeling both impatience and disappointment, she tapped her foot on the pavement. She'd just started to believe that her relationship with Stephen might actually be more than a one-way ticket down a blind alley, but now, a truckload of second thoughts crept into her mind.

"I should've known better, but oh no, not me. I had to go ahead and make a total fool of myself," she muttered to herself.

"Oh well, it doesn't matter because it's over and he's gone, probably airborn by now and headed north," she said with a sigh as she turned her back to the street sign where she'd expected to find him waiting for her.

Hearing the first wails of the police motorcade that signaled the parade was nearing its start, she steeled herself for the crowd surge that always happened as everyone jockeyed for the best spots along the parade route. She stood back not wanting to get trampled by the families who positioned their children in the front hoping they would gather sackfuls of candy and doubloons.

"Are my eyes deceiving me or can it possibly be the woman who manages to be in two places at the same time?" a gruff male voice resounded over the shrill screams of a group of excited children.

Anne thought she recognized the voice, but when she turned to see, no one was there.

"Over here, look this way," the man directed, his tone so menacing that Anne felt cold chills run down her backbone.

Spinning around, she confronted a man wearing a midnight black mask over his face. She screamed when he lunged toward her and grabbed at her throat.

"Heh, heh, nailed you, suga' foot," he said, laughing wildly.

"Taylor!" she gasped, recoiling from his squinty eyes that stared into her baby blues. "You scared me half to death. Why'd you do that?"

"I thought you needed to learn a lesson."

"What are you talking about?"

With ice in his voice, he answered, "You shouldn't have lied to me." Then he reached into his pocket and took out a chain of brightly colored beads. Wrapping them tightly around her neck, he said, "Happy Mardi Gras, lamb chop."

"Ouch, you're hurting me," she said as she strained to breathe. Suddenly she felt herself falling into the moving crush of the crowd as someone from behind pushed her to safety.

Frightened and disoriented, she heard an exchange of vile words and sinister threats between Taylor and the person who'd come to her rescue. She listened hard but because of the escalating roar of the crowd she was unable to recognize the other voice. Feeling dizzy and afraid she might lose consciousness, she dropped her head between her knees, closed her eyes, and tried to relax but her peace didn't last long.

Anne snapped to attention when she heard Taylor scream a devilish oath that made her blood curl. Glancing up, she watched him, still masked, disappear into the throng that danced ten deep on the sidewalk.

She stumbled toward the back of the crowd. As she tried to regain her composure, she searched for the best way to slip away, terrified that Taylor might reappear. She turned to leave, but she stopped in her tracks when she heard someone call her name.

"Stephen! Thank God, it's you," she said, almost fainting with relief as she fell into his arms.

Rapid fire, he said, "Don't worry, you're safe now, the bastard's gone, I promise I'll get you out of this madness."

"How did you find me?" she asked, finally relaxing enough so her heart could resume a normal rhythm.

"I just looked for the beauty who parts crowds when she passes by. Gorgeous one, that's you."

"Oh, Stephen," she replied, blushing at his exaggerated compliment.

"Are you all right?" he asked, hating that Taylor had dared to manhandle her like a piece of common trash.

"I think so," she answered, touching the pulse points in her neck. She rubbed the spots gently.

"Do you hurt there?" he asked, filled with anger for Taylor's cruel actions and mean spirit.

"Oh, Stephen, I'm fine. It was nothing really," she answered, attempting to set Stephen's mind at ease and trying to convince herself that Taylor's roughness had been an accident, a fluke. Surely he hadn't meant to harm her.

"For God's sake, Anne, I know what I saw and if I hadn't stopped that brute, he could've done some serious damage to you and no one would've been the wiser. The parade would simply have gone on."

She appreciated Stephen's concern but she felt partially responsible for Taylor's outburst. She knew she hadn't been completely honest with him, and as a result, he'd exploded.

"The man's a beast, the lowest of the low," Stephen raved, clenching his fist and narrowing his brow.

"No, he was upset," she offered in Taylor's defense. "I let him think one thing when the truth of the matter was that I didn't want to tell him that you and I were going to a dinner together. And that's all there is to it. I wasn't truthful and I got caught in my own lie."

"I don't care what you told him, Anne. He had no right to hurt you."

"He didn't really harm me, Stephen. He just doesn't know his own strength, I'm sure that's what happened."

Anne's rationalization of Taylor's actions fell on deaf ears as Stephen didn't believe one word of it, but he knew there was no convincing a woman as hard-headed as Anne.

To Anne, Taylor was a blessing, even with his faults but to Stephen, Taylor was a black spot in the universe. At a stalemate on the point, they agreed to an unspoken truce.

"Let's go back to the parade," Anne said, reaching for Stephen's hand.

"I'm with you," he answered. Finding a break in the crowd close to the sidewalk, he stood behind Anne so she'd have the best view of the floats that were fast approaching their corner.

"Look at that, I don't believe it. This is amazing!" he yelled above the din of the crowd.

Anne laughed at the delight she heard in his voice and saw written over his face when a huge float headed their way. "Here comes the emblem float," she explained. "The first one always carries the insignia of the mystic society that's parading."

"Incredible," he said, fascinated by the ornate crest of two peacocks grasping silken ribbons that spun in the center of the float. "What's it mean?" he shouted.

"That's the crest of La Femme d'Societie," she answered. "They've..." She'd intended to tell him the history of the group, but she had to hold her thoughts--he evidently had something else on his mind and parade pagentry wasn't it.

As everyone in the crowd waved their arms high above their heads and begged for treats from the maskers riding aboard the lighted float, Stephen turned Anne toward him and lifted her into his arms. He kissed her tenderly and loved her with his eyes.

A marching band passed and then a drill team from Saraland. Oblivious to both groups, Stephen tightened his arms around her petite and perfect body. He wished he could hold her forever, but reality set in--he was booked on the 9:50 flight to Washington National, a plane he had to catch if he wanted to keep his job. Reluctantly, he released Anne from his tender hold.

She touched her kiss-swollen lips, locking into her mind exactly how she felt at that moment--loved, wanted, sexy. She wished she could always feel that way. Then she decided she had to make the best of her last hours with Stephen.

She wanted him to leave Mobile with nothing less than memories of a wonderful, happy time.

Smiling bravely, she watched the next float round the corner. "Oh, look Stephen, this one depicts La Femme's theme for Mardi Gras."

"An extravaganza on wheels," he said, as he watched a massive float careen toward them. He couldn't believe the sight before his eyes. Under the glare of floodlights from WALA-TV 10, two dozen La Femmes, wearing costumes of satin and sequins, gyrated like crazed kids to the driving beat of a "truck band" combo that played a strange mix of selections ranging from "Cheeseburger in Paradise" to reggae. Amazed at the sight of grown women who seemed delighted to shimmy and shake around an animated dancing top hat, he turned to Anne and asked, "Care to explain this one?"

"Look at the banner on the side of the float," she replied as she nodded toward a splash of neon lettering that was highlighted by thousands of silver sequins.

"Top Hat Review," he read. "Must be an awards show."

"I think you're right," she said. Then giggling, she added, "I bet they give 'The Most Gracious Woman's Society Award' to themselves." She laughed at the thought.

Stephen loved watching Anne, her excitement was contagious. Entertained by her running commentary on the parade, he followed her instructions about proper parade etiquette. When she said, "Go high," he did, and when she said, "Grab it," he followed her orders, straining to snag the throws hurled from the floats.

"What are we catching? Anything in particular?" Stephen asked a man standing to his left.

Struggling to balance a blond toddler on his shoulders, the man answered, "I tell you what, you take anything they throw out and be glad you caught it. My boy, here, loves everything."

"Okay, I'm a player," Stephen responded and he kept his word. Toy cigars, commemorative doubloons, bubblegum, streamers, you name it and Stephen Richards extended his tall frame above the masses to shag everything that came within his reach.

Anne also did her fair share of catching as she snagged a couple of stuffed animals and handfuls of candy treats. Together their haul was complete, most of which they shared with the father and son standing beside them.

More bands played on and more marchers strutted, but then another float turned the corner. Seeing it approach, a roar came up from the crowd--"Beads, more beads. We want beads and moon pies. Moon pies. Here! Here!"

"What are they saying?" Stephen asked, needing a quick translation.

"The crowd's begging for the maskers to throw more beaded necklaces and moon pies--you know, those cookie-like things that are filled with gooey marshmallow." She waited for him to respond but when she saw him draw a blank, she asked, "Do you know what I'm talking about?"

"Not really," he answered, shaking his head at the concept.

"Moon pies are a Mardi Gras tradition in Mobile," she said. "They're covered either in chocolate, banana, or..."

Her explanation ended abruptly when a very well-endowed and snuggly shrimp-costumed La Femme, swaying precariously on the top level of the "Best Food on the Gulf Coast" float, shouted, "Stephen! Look up, over here. It's me."

"Didn't I tell you? There's Big Moo, posing for everyone to behold," Anne said, grimacing as she saw Brandie Sue wink and smile at Stephen.

"This is for you, handsome, a special delivery message for your eyes only," Brandie Sue yelled as she threw a golden streamer that landed at Stephen's feet.

"Go ahead, read it, I know you want to," Anne said, encouraging Stephen to satisfy his, and her, curiosity.

He unrolled the banner and read the message. Folding it back up, he shook his head and chuckled.

"Come on, what did Miss Brandie Sue say? Tell me." Anne felt her good humor dissipate.

"It was nothing, just something about power, motion, sex, and me. That's all."

"That's all? Don't you get it? She's propositioning you, and from a float at Mardi Gras. Of all the nerve," Anne fumed.

Reacting quickly to Anne's interpretation of Brandie Sue's note, Stephen leaned down and kissed Anne quiet.

Whispering, "Simmer down," he held her until he felt her unclench her fists. Then he said, "She's nothing to me. I care only about you, not her."

"Well, well, Annie doll, you know better than to believe a damn Yankee," boomed a voice above the raucous noise of the crowd.

Stephen turned quickly in the direction of the voice he was learning to hate and cursed at the sight of his nemesis striding boldly toward Anne.

"This is for you, baby cakes, please forgive me," Taylor said as he placed a large, velvety box into Anne's shaking hands.

With her heart pounding, she said. "Forget it, Taylor. You just got carried away." Looking at him with forgiveness and understanding in her eyes, she added, "I should've told you the truth last night. I honestly didn't mean to hurt you."

"Nor I you," Taylor responded as he awkwardly embraced Anne against his chubby frame.

Stephen, having seen and heard enough, coughed rudely and said, "Excuse me, I don't mean to interrupt, but...,"

"What do you want?" Taylor asked as he narrowed his small eyes at Stephen. He seemed determined to keep the momentum going in his favor. Turning his back on Stephen and positioning himself between Stephen and Anne, he encouraged her to open his gift.

Being a true Southern woman able to spot a jewelry box a mile away, Anne glanced down, feeling decidedly uncomfortable with the nature of his present. With polite hesitation in her voice, she asked, "Here, Taylor? With all these strangers milling around?"

She waited for his reply, feeling her skin crawl with dread as she worried what strings were attached to his gift.

"Go ahead, open it, sweet pea. I'll play bodyguard if it'll make you feel better," he said, leering at her through his heavily shaded, half-closed eyes.

Stephen didn't know whether to throw a punch or throw up, but he was certain about one thing--if any man was going to protect Anne, he was going to do the honors. Taylor might try to buy her affection, but Stephen was going straight for her heart.

"Oh, look. How beautiful," Anne said, momentarily dazzled by Taylor's gift of a triple strand pearl choker that he hastily clasped around her neck. Wanting to oblate from Anne's mind the memory of his earlier roughness, he placed the necklace around her throat as gently as his pudgy fingers would allow.

The icy touch of his hands sent shivers up and down Anne's spine and her fear of him resurfaced when she felt the pearls rub against her pulse points that Taylor had pressed so abrasively earlier.

She swallowed hard and said, "You're very kind, but I can't accept this gift." When she tried to remove the choker, Taylor stilled her movement by grabbing her wrists.

"No, no, ducky dear, this time I have to insist." He wasn't about to add rejection to his list of grievances. "Come on, suga' lips, humor an ol' pal and we'll forget our misunderstandin's and start over."

Realizing that any further discussion was pointless, she gave in, saying, "All right, but you know this gift wasn't necessary." Turning to Stephen, she asked, "Did you see what he gave me?"

"Impossible to miss," he replied. "I guess they're not faux gems." Stephen had to give Taylor credit for his excellent taste in jewels, but he wished that Taylor's intentions for Anne were as flawless as the pearls that complemented the luster of her delicate complexion.

"Well, well, here we are, the three of us together, just like the other night," Taylor said, whistling through his cosmetically bleached teeth. "So, Stephen, ol' boy, are you waitin' for the parade to end so you can meet up with that buxom lass I saw blowin' you kisses or are you just killin' time?"

Time wasn't what Stephen wanted to kill. Frowning, he replied, "I'm here with Anne, we were enjoying the parade, that is, until you..."

Whispering low so only Stephen could hear, Taylor bragged, "She's mine and I'm here to claim her." He grinned smuggly, believing he'd just won another victory. Elated that Anne now wore his trademark gift that he presented to his high-class conquests, he felt confident that she'd never find out that he kept a ready supply of triple-strand pearl necklaces on hand, just in case.

Wanting to deflate Taylor's ego and warn Anne at the same time, Stephen turned to her and said, "I couldn't help but notice that you have a pretty impressive library of ancient literature. Remember the epic about the Trojan horse?"

Taylor, bristling like a banty rooster, preened forward and said, "So, Stevie, are you sayin' you've been inside Annie's home? Do anything besides read her book titles?"

"At least I can read," Stephen replied, brushing up against Taylor and staring coldly into his bloodshot eyes.

"Hey, fellows," Anne interjected, "Mardi Gras is a time to celebrate--so let's concentrate on the fun all around us." Not wanting to witness another shouting match between the two men, she traded positions with Taylor so that she stood in the middle. On her right, handsome and suave Stephen scowled and on her left, moody yet sometimes charming Taylor sulked.

"What am I going to do with you two?" she asked, looking first from one to the other.

Although opposite in appearance, mannerisms, and needs, the two men agreed on one subject--they both desired Anne, but in different ways. One wanted to marry her and give her the world; the other, having already pirated away her world, wanted to possess her and hoard his bounty.

"Well, pretty puss, it seems to me that you won't have the problem much longer. What time does your big bird fly, Stevie boy?" Taylor asked gleefully.

Anne glanced down at her feet, saddened by the thought of Stephen's leaving her. She wondered if she'd ever see him again. Then she remembered that he'd assured her that she would never regret their closeness--she clung to that thought, wanting to trust him and believing there was something special about him that made him stand apart from other men.

"Cheer up, cream puff, look what's headin' our way," Taylor said as he grabbed at Anne's chin, forcing her to face the street.

Her eyes widened in surprise as she watched a costumed rider on a black stallion charge toward them. Wearing a silk diamond-pattered outfit that gleamed in the street lights, the masked man turned his horse toward the corner where Anne stood anchored between Stephen and Taylor.

Pulling tightly on his horse's reins, the masker made his heavily breathing mount rear on its hind legs in front of Stephen. With hatred clouding his weasel-like eyes, the rider shouted, "Hey, bubba! In your face," and hurled a huge moon pie at Stephen that sharply bounced off his chest before it fell to the ground.

Turning toward Anne, Stephen said, "I thought you said all this was in fun. That idiot just about drilled a hole through my heart."

"What flavor's your prize, Stevie?" Taylor asked with a shifty glint in his eyes.

"There's one way to find out," Stephen said as he tore off the silver foil wrapper, "Banana. Are you happy?" he answered, breaking the moon pie into thirds to share.

Anne gasped and put her hand to her mouth. "Don't touch that!" she screamed.

Not understanding her reaction, Stephen held the moon pie pieces in his left hand and reached for Anne with his right. "What's wrong?"

Terror silenced her vocal cords, allowing her only to point at Stephen's hand with disgust.

Seeing vile bits of fish guts oozing from the center of the moon pie, Stephen shook his head in revulsion. "What the hell? Is this someone's idea of a sick joke?" he asked, glaring in Taylor's direction. Then to Anne, who was visibly shaken by the sight, he said, "Forget this insanity, whoever did this needs serious help."

"Looks like it's one of a kind, maybe a collector's item. You oughtta keep it next to your heart as a souvenir," Taylor suggested as he watched Stephen reach for an empty container that someone had discarded on the sidewalk.

"Very funny, pal," Stephen replied, but he wasn't laughing. "This is pure trash."

Anne couldn't find the words to express her anguish that Stephen's first Mobile Mardi Gras parade was ending so badly. Sensing her concern, he winked at her and said, "Don't give this idiocy another thought. Every town has its share of characters and I guess I just ran into one tonight."

"Sounds like you're not very superstitious or maybe you just don't know what receivin' a sign like that means," Taylor said, faking a smile.

Stephen wasn't stupid. He knew full well the implications, the threat. Even so, he didn't see any benefit in analyzing the hows and whys, at least not in front of a gloating Taylor and a frightened Anne.

Taylor slapped Stephen on the back and howled with derisive laughter. He said something to Anne, but sirens from a police motorcade drowned out his words.

"That's the end of the parade, it's over," Anne said, looking longingly at Stephen.

"I'll walk you to your car," he said, feeling very empty inside but knowing the time had come for him to leave Mobile. Dismissing Taylor with an abrupt nod, he took Anne by the arm and led her away, leaving Taylor standing alone on the sidewalk that was littered from one end to the other with candy wrappers, smashed beads, torn streamers, and empty cups and cans.

Anne looked over her shoulder and tossed Taylor a fleeting, farewell smile.

"Don't worry about him, he'll be fine," Stephen said stonily. "He's a survivor, but I'm not so sure how I'm going to manage without you," he added as they approached the lot where she'd left her car. "Will you miss me?"

"Of course, I will," she answered as they shared one last bittersweet kiss.

Stephen was a man accustomed to deadlines and departures, but this time pulled him apart. He promised Anne that he would call, and often. Sighing, he said, "I'd give anything to steal away with you to your beach haven, but..."

"Don't say anything else. I know how you feel, but..." she replied.

They stood locked together in a long and loving embrace, their hearts joined but breaking.

Pulling back, Stephen looked into Anne's eyes and her soul. "I promise you won't be sorry that we met. I'll call you as soon as I can." He kissed her lightly and brushed away the tears that streaked down her cheeks.

And then he was gone and she was alone, or at least she thought she was.

"Hey, suga' doll. Don't you fret, I'm right here, ready and willin' to bring sunshine back to your life. Come here and let me make it all better."

"Taylor Hamilton, you're just everywhere tonight," she said, actually glad he'd followed her. Her heart ached so badly that she hoped his comforting words would soothe her broken spirit.

"Better let this traffic clear out of town. I know a warm, cozy spot where we can talk while we wait. Believe it or not, I am a real good listener," he said, liking the idea of not having to share Anne, his parade prize, with anyone.

Realizing that she needed a friend, she decided that no harm could come from her spending an hour or two with Taylor so she said, "Okay, lead the way." Her mind wandered to thoughts of Stephen as she blindly followed behind Taylor who strode on ahead like a king leading a grand march.

"The Master King, I am, I am," he sang under his breath, smiling broadly as he mentally congratulated himself on his fine work. Two times that night he'd placed Anne in the position where she'd had to decide either to see things his way or not, and in both instances she'd wavered to his side. He liked that kind of control--to him that meant she was manageable.

Although he sensed that she had something sexual going with Stephen, Taylor blew it off as hormonal infatuation that would soon be yesterday's news, especially since Stephen was finally out of the picture.

"Hey dumplin', step along now. We're almost at Crawdaddy's Bar and Grill. You're lookin' kinda peaked, like maybe you could use a beer and some crab cakes. Just the thing to bring you around, especially since you've got an appointment tomorrow."

"What did you say?" she asked.

"Oh, that's right, sunshine, I'd planned to tell you last night over dinner at the Malaga Inn, but...well, you know what happened to our date."

She blushed, ashamed for her dishonesty.

"Are you sorry you treated ol' Taylor so bad?" He studied her face, enjoying the guilt he saw flicker in her eyes.

"I'm sorry, Taylor. I apologize."

"Does that mean that you're gonna be a good girl and do as I say?"

"Taylor!" she answered, wanting to chastise him for his condescending tone but afraid to anger him.

"Since I've such a big heart, love dove, I'll forgive you-- you bad, bad girl." He snorted like a pig and then said, "I'll tell you the deal. I know someone who wants to see your resume, soon, like tomorrow. I'll give you the scoop when we get to Crawdaddy's."

She felt her heart skip a beat, relieved that she had a chance to start over, both with a job interview and with Taylor. Thinking, he's really not so bad, she stood taller and walked faster in order to match his pace.

"Oopsie doodle, doll face, hold on to me and watch out for that big ol' streetsweeper headin' our way. I'm real glad to see it comin' down the road, it's time for all the trash to be thrown out of our town." Thinking about Stephen, he made a fist and then grinned.

Taylor could barely contain his joy. Anne was on his arm and he believed he was on his way to another successful merger. Life was good and he was ready to reap the rewards of the black seeds he'd sown.

Pushing his way into Crawdaddy's, he led Anne to a back table in the crowded bar that was filled with seedy back alley types who smelled of cigarette smoke and stale beer. Noticing that Anne turned up her nose in displeasure, Taylor took her hand and said, "It's awful at first I know, but after a while you'll get used to the smell. Trust me, this is an okay place, the food's good, too, you'll see, honey lips."

Anne shook her head, seriously doubting Taylor's prediction and thinking about Stephen. She knew he would never take her to such a dump and she wondered why Taylor had.

"Thinkin' about Mr. High and Mighty?" Taylor asked. "Now Anne, I haven't had a lot of relationships," he said, lying like a dog, "so I'm no authority, but I could see right off that you and that sanctimonious piece of...well, anyway, believe me, it wouldn't have worked. Your backgrounds are too different, you're too classy for that loser. Besides, buttercup, you need a real man who can showcase your talents."

"Do you have someone in mind?" she asked, disliking Taylor's unsolicited, but persistent, attacks on Stephen.

He licked his thick lips and smiled, "Yes, as a matter of fact I do. He's like me, a winner, a champ." He leaned toward her and placed his clammy hands on her shoulders and pulled her closer.

Changing the subject quickly, she squirmed in her chair in order to avoid his hot breath that made the fine hairs on the back of her neck stand up. "Who wants to see my resume?"

"A man with a lot to offer, but you'd probably have to move from here."

"Where, Taylor?" she asked, hating the thought of relocation.

"Atlanta, beauty belle, that's where the jobs are. In fact, I've got a spot waitin' for you in my shop if you'll only sign on the dotted line. Salary and perks are negotiable," he said, leering at her as though she was a Porterhouse steak.

"It's out of the question, Taylor. I meant what I said about my grandfather needing me. That part was the truth." Anne looked him straight in the eye so he would have no doubts about her sincerity.

"Too bad, blue eyes, we could make a dynamite team. But if you're gonna be stubborn, I guess I'll just have to let you talk to this other man about a VP slot that's opened. Big bucks, I'm sure."

Anne sighed, her emotions torn between appreciation for his concern for her well-being, fear of his temper, and guilt for having misled him. Touching the pearl choker he'd insisted she wear, she felt even guiltier. "Taylor, when you want to, you can be one of the kindest guys I've ever known. I can't tell you how much your friendship means to me."

"Go on, darlin', try."

"Oh, Taylor, you know what I mean, I value knowing you and not just because of your success...,"

"Uh oh, I think I hear a 'but' comin'," he said, covering her hand with slobbery kisses.

Flinching, she said, "But for our friendship to work, I think we need to be totally honest with one another. I'll do my part from now on."

"And you know you can count on me. Remember our friends called me 'Taylor the Honest Hamilton' for a reason." He waited for her to reply but when she remained silent, he added, "Surely you haven't forgotten how I was always the bravest of the bunch."

She thought for a moment and said, "You mean when you showed no fear kidnapping our housemother?"

"Yes, and what else do you remember about me?" he asked, totally self-consumed.

"And then there was your reputation as the..."

"Best man around town," he said, bragging and patting his groin. "Oh, yeah," he added, "'Mr. Wonderful,' that's what all the girls called me, you know."

"What?"

"You heard me, I was 'Mr. Wonderful' then and I still am but now I'm huntin' for 'Ms. Wonderful.'" He winked at Anne, thinking, that's you, sweet cakes, with some alterations here and there, of course--I'm gonna make you my wife.

"I hope you find her," Anne said. "You deserve happiness."

"Well, so do you, pussy foot, but that Richards clown's not your type."

Frowning, Anne asked, "How do you know that?"

Taylor reached around and patted Anne's behind, saying, "Trust ol' Taylor, you don't need a wimp like that weak stick."

"Taylor!" she objected, swatting away his fat hands that clumsily stroked her back.

"Well, excuse me, love locks, but you've got to admit he handled that whole moon pie thing like a sissy, so neat and all, the way he threw it away like a prissy grandma. If that'd been me, I woulda taken that sucker and shoved it up that horseman's..."

"That's enough," she said, standing up, ready to leave.

Yanking her to her chair, Taylor grinned like a wolverine that had just spotted its dinner.

She blanked all thoughts of Taylor out of her mind and allowed pure thoughts of Stephen to wash over her psyche. She saw him as kind and sensitive, a real man whose strength allowed him to have a softer side. In her mind, that wasn't weakness.

"About time they brought our damn dinner," Taylor said, pinching the waitress as she tried to sneak by his chair.

Having lost her appetite, Anne watched Taylor gorge mounds of crab cakes into his big mouth. She turned her face away, unable to watch him wash his dinner down with a pitcher of dark, frothy beer.

Instead, she looked out the front window, lost in her memories of her night of passion with Stephen that she feared would never be repeated.

Taylor, assuming Anne was being respectful of his need to eat his meal in peace, thought about himself, his past conquests. Yes, indeed, he mused, this king's ready to crown a new queen, so she'd best get ready, 'cause here I come, rammin' through.

A mile high in the air, Stephen sensed that Anne was thinking about him. Wanting to tell her how much he cared for her--no, he thought, that's not it, I want to tell her that I love her--he asked a flight attendant to bring him an airphone. After repeated, futile tries to connect with Anne, he gave up calling and stared blankly out the window.

"Can I get you something else, sir?" the attendant asked as she passed by him. Nodding toward the tray of drinks she carried, she suggested, "A martini, perhaps?"

"No, thanks, ma'am. What I need is unobtainable. Unfortunately for me, she's miles away and not answering her phone."

"Sorry," the attendant said, shaking her head sympathetically. Walking to the back of the cabin, she whispered to her crew chief, "Check out the hunk in 2A, a man in love with a woman who probably doesn't know her own good fortune."

"Where are you, Anne Livingston?" Stephen muttered to himself, wishing he could hear her sweet voice one more time.

"What are you thinkin', angel lips?" Taylor asked, determined to bring Anne back to their conversation. Not liking the way her mind seemed to wander, he decided that was something else he would get her to work on. Distracting quirks simply didn't fit into his master plan--that sort of unacceptable behavior could cause a dinner party to fail and that wasn't Taylor Hamilton's style.

"Oh, Taylor, sorry, I don't mean to be rude. I'm just a bit tired."

"Hey, your buddy Taylor understands. A bit of beauty rest should help. After all, we've got a big day ahead of us, sweetie pie." Nothing clouded his mind--he knew exactly where he was headed.

"What are you talking about?"

"We're goin' on a road trip, baby doll, you need a vacation from your worries. Tell you how it is, we'll buzz by a board meetin' at Bellingrath Gardens first, then we're gonna go on to Biloxi for a night of fun. You do want to follow up on that job interview, don't you?"

"Sure I do," she answered, beaming at him with hope in her heart that she stood a chance professionally after all. "Thank goodness my navy suit's clean," she said, planning her wardrobe for the next day.

Taylor smiled slyly and said, "And don't forget that low-cut hot pink number I saw hangin' in your closet. You'll need it at the casino." He rubbed his chubby hands together, pleased that his plan was cooking.

Anne smiled at him, unaware that she was about to become the main ingredient in his steaming cauldron of lies and deceit.

CHAPTER 11

"You're waking up to Coast 100. Hello, Mobile and Pensacola--we're gonna rock today." Recognizing the voices of the morning WMXC deejays, Beau and Cheri, Anne sat up in bed. Stretching, she tried to pull herself out of her deep but very troubled sleep that had been riddled with replays of the night before.

She reached for Bella who snuggled close beside her. Stroking Bella's soft fur, she listened to her cat's rhythmic purring and remembered the sounds that had rumbled from deep inside Stephen when she'd rubbed against his chest hairs the first time.

Missing him terribly, she felt drained of all excitement, all joy. "What's wrong with me?" she cried, hearing the Eagles' refrain "Get over it! Get over it!" blare from her radio.

"I wish I could," she said as she forced herself to face her immediate situation. She knew she should feel totally ecstatic to have a chance to land another job, but she couldn't seem to get herself motivated in that direction. Instead, she fell back into her pillows, limp as a rag doll, not wanting to leave the nest of her bed.

She glanced at her clock and shook her head with disbelief. "Oh dear, Bella, it's late. I've got so much to do if I'm going to impress Taylor's friend." Looking at herself in the mirror, she quickly turned away and said with a sigh of disgust, "There's no hope. I might as well forget the whole thing."

"Get it in gear, pretty woman! It's a bright new day and we've got a date."

Anne jumped as though she'd touched a live wire. "Taylor? Taylor Hamilton? Is that you?" she asked, turning toward the sound of his voice. "Why are you in my house?" she asked, rubbing her eyes. She grabbed her robe and quickly threw it over her worn flannel pajamas.

"Look at you, fancy pants, I never figured you for a woodsy type."

"Fooled you then, Taylor. But let me ask you one more time--why are you in my house?"

He folded his arms around his wide girth and chuckled, "Cranky, too--my, my, mornin' glory, you're a woman of many emotions. Good thing I like a filly with feelin's."

"What are you talking about? And why are you standing in my bedroom?"

"Impatient, too. Well, now, I guess you don't remember everything that happened after we left Crawdaddy's," he replied as he gave her a knowing wink and left her, totally mystified, sitting on her bed.

"Wait a minute, Taylor, come back here. I want the truth, now."

Leering around the door, he asked, "What's to explain, Annie pie? You just got a little tired and asked me to stay over. That's all," he said, gloating like a honeymooner.

"I did no such thing," she swore, adding, "you're wrong. I would've remembered something like that."

Turning toward her bed, he reached to the left side and picked up a flattened pillow. "You really should upgrade these. I prefer Beautyrest queen size and heavy on the stuffing, not like this pitiful lump you sleep on, honey pot."

Stunned by his words, she gulped and tried to take an offensive stance, "Thanks for sharing, Taylor, but I really can't see myself buying pillows for your head right now."

"Is that so? Could've fooled me last night, butter puss." He smiled broadly as he watched her grimace.

Anne paced around her room and said, "You're crazy, Taylor. What are you insinuating? That I asked you to spend the night and you did?"

"Bingo and give the lovely lady a silver dollar," he replied, patting his heart with one hand and fanning his upper thighs with the other.

"Oh, no, oh, no!" Anne said, shaking her head in denial. She felt her anxiety level shoot up 1,000 points as she maintained emphatically, "You're off base, Taylor. I didn't invite you into either my home or my bed."

"Au contraire, butterfly, the truth is that right before you dozed off in my car..."

"Your car?" she asked, collapsing into her mattress.

"Yes, my car. I had it brought around to Crawdaddy's, it saved us havin' to walk back uptown to yours, darlin'."

Anne gulped, struggling with her emotions that engulfed her.

"It's God's truth, kissy face--you begged me to stay with you. I asked you about our sleepin' arrangements but you closed your baby blues and were gone, down for the count. I figured you must not've slept much the night before. What wore you out so, angel face?"

Blushing, she recalled every vivid, intoxicating detail of the night she and Stephen had shared--a night for the record books she'd never imagined possible. But now, he was gone and she was alone, except for Bella and Taylor, who seemed too much at ease in her bedroom.

Taylor ignored Anne's flushed face, writing it off as "female trouble." Thinking, drugs can take care of that little problem, he concentrated on a more pressing concern. "Did you know that you talk in your sleep?" he asked, tugging on the sash of her robe.

Although filled with dread for what her subconscious might've given away, she replied bravely, "Tell me what I said." Holding her breath, she tightened her robe around her waist and waited.

Taylor flopped down on her bed and leaned his large head toward her. Patting her on the knee, he said, "Suga' cookie, you talked a blue streek, callin' me 'star man' and 'love pistol.' Then you started moanin', 'more love, give it to me, give it to me.' I swear, love lumps, listenin' to you got me so hot that I had to stop the damn car."

"You what?" she gasped.

"You heard me, honey lips. How could I turn a deaf ear to a beggin' babe? I'm not crazy, you know, so I did like any other red-blooded bubba--I parked the car where we could have some privacy, if you know what I mean, sweet cheeks."

The remembrance of Taylor's hot, sour breath washed sickeningly over Anne. All she could manage was a faint gasp although her brain screamed, "Please tell me it isn't so!"

"The rest is as we say history. I knew we were pretty good friends, angel baby, but I had no idea how much you cared about me." He licked his lips and trailed a line of sloppy kisses around her mouth and down her chin. When he finished, he grabbed at her hair and asked, "So tell me, wild woman, don't you think it's about time for you to drop your coy bit and admit to ol' Taylor that I'm your love man?"

Anne shivered, filled with revulsion and regret and praying that she hadn't slept with him--she knew who made her shake to her toes and that person wasn't Taylor Hamilton. But then, she wondered, what if I actually gave my love to Taylor that I meant for Stephen? Her mind raced with the possibility that maybe Taylor spoke the truth, he sounded so convincing. If so, she would have to deal with the consequences of a gigantic mistake.

Taylor jabbed at Anne's nose and said, "Still wanna smell my maleness?"

Appalled and sickened to her stomach at the thought, she screamed, "Taylor, I have to sort all this out. I value our friendship but that's the sum total of our relationship. We're friends, pals, buddies, that's it."

"Close personal friends is more the way I see it, thunder thighs," he answered, stroking her hair in a familiar way that made her flesh crawl.

Feeling a sudden need to take a hot shower, she bolted toward the bathroom, determined to scrub away all remnants of Taylor's touch. "Did we kiss?" she asked as she snatched up a three-pack of Ivory and a bottle of Listerine.

"Repeatedly and with feeling, wild thing," he answered with a smirk in his voice.

Anne had heard enough, so much so that she felt she might spontaneously combust. She simply couldn't handle the possibility that she'd become involved with Taylor when she knew her heart belonged to Stephen, the only man who'd ever made her earth spin. She cleared her throat and said, "We'll talk about this later, Taylor,"

"Don't worry about talkin', baby doll. We're way beyond that stage in buildin' our love nest. I'll give you everything you've ever wanted, you won't be sorry. We'll turn this town around, just you wait and see. But for now, I need to go back to my place for a change of clothes. We have a date at Bellingrath Gardens so I want to look good for you. Don't stray off, cuddlekins, 'cause I'm comin' right back."

He laughed all the way to his car, thinking, little Anne's so gullible. Chuckling, he decided he'd let her believe a few kisses had led to much more although she'd been so deeply asleep that it would've taken a steam engine to arouse her. "You took my bait deep, darlin'," he said, "now I just have to reel you in--my prize catch." Congratulating himself on his victory, he prepared for his next move.

He stormed into his penthouse and stalked into his dressing room. Shuffling through row after row of hand-tailored garments that lined his walk-in closet, he grabbed a double-breasted black suit and grinned. "Yeah, I like this one," he spoke to his reflection in the mirror. "Screams money and position, two objects I dearly love."

Thinking how Anne would look on his arm as they crossed the bridge over Mirror Lake at Bellingrath Gardens, Taylor smirked, proud of all the choices he'd made lately. He knew he'd tapped the mother lode when he'd planted expansion plans in the midmanagement minds at Livingston Enterprises and then had used insider information to set the timetable for his slow but steady buyout of first one division and then another. "Good work, Taylor, you stud god," he shouted as he lumbered across the room to the bar.

He toasted his success with a double shot of vodka, all the while laughing at Anne for unwittingly falling into his trap that'd taken her company as well as her fortune. Thinking, too bad, Annie doll, that your expansion bucks extended your debt over the danger zone--a move that killed you but helped me, making me rich and richer. "It's mine, now, all mine," he crowed.

Selecting a Jerry Garcia tie, he held it against his suit and smiled. "Perfect," he said, kissing the air with his fat lips. "Just like my plan--golden. It's off the drawin' board and rollin' on. So what Ms. Anniepuss doesn't wanna go to Atlanta? Maybe I'll just set her up with a lil' business in Mobile. Commutin's not really so bad, gives me latitude to do what I please without worryin' about a poutin' ball and chain."

He struggled into his suit coat, cursing the tailor for his bad measurements. "What the hell," he said, "Anne can bust her buns playin' corporate head a few days a week, then I'll bust her sweet butt playin' house with me on the weekends. What a life!--a dream come true," he added, lusting at the thought of all the wine and women he could consume during the work week while Anne toiled hundreds of miles away.

The more he thought about the assets Anne offered to him as his wife, the more excited he became about the final piece of his grand scheme. Before the night was over, she would be his.

Whistling "Dixie," he showered and shaved. He dressed quickly and then rushed to make some calls before he picked up Anne for their drive to Theodore.

"Jerry, Taylor Hamilton here, I need somethin', fast. 18K settin', 4-5 carats, radiant cut." He paused, listening only for a second before he erupted with a foul oath. "Look here, you dumb #!*@, I don't give a *#!@ about your sources. Just get it to me tonight, no later than 8:30. Messenger it to the Dixie Gambler at Biloxi. Use the TMK account."

He slammed down the receiver, muttering, "*#!@ moron." He shook his head in disgust and said, "Next," as he placed another call.

"Carson, Taylor Hamilton. She's ready to talk job but make her sweat so it'll seem real. Go easy on the perks--I don't want her thinkin' she's some big deal. Yeah, kinda like that other 'liberated' female we put the squeeze to," he said, snorting into the phone. "Hell man, you and I know what these skirts really want." He paused, howling like a coyote, and then said, "We're set for dinner at the Table Round in Biloxi at 7 tonight."

Another call, and that'll be a wrap, he thought, as he slicked back his hair and plopped into a chair.

"Matt, Taylor Hamilton. Any word on that sleaze Richards? What? He's clean? Can't be, you'd best keep on diggin'. I know the dirt's there so unearth it, boy. And now! Do you understand?"

Taylor slammed the receiver down, furious that Stephen's reputation appeared flawless. Gritting his teeth, he growled and then grinned, saying, "Not for long, Stevie boy. All it'll take are a few words in the right ears and then Anne'll hate your guts."

He licked his lips, thinking about nibbling on Anne's little ears and her royal neck. "Ha! Ha!" he yelled, slapping his ample thigh. "That's it. Go for broke, studman."

He pictured the perfect scene--Anne nodding her head, "Yes," as he placed a diamond ring on her finger. He knew she was such a traditionalist about right and wrong that she'd accept his proposal, especially since she believed she'd compromised her virtue with him. But then he frowned, thinking that she might balk because of her infatuation with Stephen. Angry, he pounded his fist on a table and vowed, "Hell with that, Annie poo, I'll fix that problem fast with a little help from the home front." Gleefully he reached for the phone to make one last call.

"You heard me, bring him to the Bellingrath House at 2:30, sharp. Do this right, Todd, and a Z-28 may be in your future."

Taylor considered calling Anne to sweet-talk her into a more receptive mood for his advances. Then he remembered her phone wouldn't ring since he'd silenced it with a flip of the switch the night before. He hadn't wanted any interruptions from the outside, especially not from Stephen.

He mopped his brow with a silk handkerchief, hoping she hadn't checked her phone's operation. Stalking around the room, he said, "Hell, if she does, I'll blame it on her damn cat. That critter's a nuisance. Needs to be eliminated just like Stevie boy. Yes indeed, sent airborn with a one-way ticket and no return scheduled."

Toying with a cup of coffee, Anne stared dejectedly at her telephone. She leaned against her kitchen sink and wondered why Stephen hadn't called as he'd promised.

Bella rubbed against her ankle, meowing pitifully.

"Are you sad, too?" Anne asked, lifting Bella into her arms and turning away from her phone. "Let's get out of here, little cat. There's no use hanging around hoping he'll call. I guess he's forgotten about me, otherwise..." Her mind drifted back to their night at the beach, it'd been heaven on earth for her and she'd thought he'd felt the same way. "Guess not," she said, feeling her heart turn to stone.

She forced herself to complete her basic grooming. Staring blankly into her bathroom mirror, she frowned as she brushed her hair, wondering what had happened to its shine, its life.

"So be it," she said, winding her hair into a sensible knot. "I'd better get my mind on my interview and off of Stephen. He's gone and that's the bottom line." Then her mind flashed a picture of Taylor leering at her. She flinched and shuddered at the thought although she knew she should try to think positively about him.

How wonderful that he arranged this appointment for me, she mused, but then she frowned, thinking how much more wonderful life would be if she were with Stephen instead. She closed her eyes and imagined him toweling her off after a shower. Smiling, she felt better but then her mind flipflopped Stephen's handsome face for Taylor's toothy grin. She screamed and dropped her brush as though she was holding a snake.

The crash made Bella leap from her perch on top of the bath vanity. Letting out a frightened howl, she hid behind the sink and covered her eyes with her furry paws.

"Come here, baby, a nightmare just raced through me," Anne said as she bent over to retrieve her brush that had skidded across the tile floor. She stood up and ran her hands over her stomach and down her thighs as if to reassure herself that she was just as Stephen had left her.

Praying that Taylor hadn't touched her, she tried to dismiss her fear that things had gotten out of hand with him. She hadn't intended to mislead him, but if she had, she didn't believe that he would've retaliated by taking advantage of her. Taylor's not perfect, she reasoned, but still he's a born and bred Southerner, a gentleman at heart. She raised her eyes heavenward, thinking, please send me a sign so I'll know that's true.

She waited for something miraculous to happen, but when nothing did, she shrugged her shoulders and said, "Oh well, I can't change the past, but at least I can set Taylor straight tonight."

With a worried frown creasing her brow, she put the final touches on her all-business attire and readied herself for her day and evening with Taylor. She folded her pink cocktail dress neatly and placed it in an overnight bag along with silk hose and satin pumps.

She glanced at her telephone, still wanting to hear Stephen's voice before she left. "I'll call his office," she said, but then she shook her head, thinking, no, I'd better not, the last thing he needs is a woman chasing him. Anyway, he's probably busy, she rationalized, as she pictured him facing a backlog of paperwork.

She knew how a stack of paper could seem to grow into a mound almost overnight. Remembering that she used to have that problem, she sighed. Then she resolved that she would fight for her career and her company. "It's not over yet," she pledged, thinking, Livingston Enterprises might be a dead issue on the NASDAQ list, but to me, it's still alive.

To regain control, she knew she needed to reestablish her credibility. With that thought in mind, Anne turned on her PC and keyed in her resume. As she watched her printer feed out two copies, she kept one eye on the mounting paper stack and the other on the telephone. "Come on, ring, now," she implored the block of plastic that sat like a silent sentry. "What's wrong with you, anyway?" she asked, picking up her phone.

She lifted the receiver and listened to the dial tone. "It's connected," she said, but then she looked at the phone's base. Thinking, how strange, she stared at the ringer switch.

"Bella, get in here. Did you do this?" she asked her cat who replied with a look of wide-eyed innocence.

"The 'ringer off' button's pushed in. Wonder how that happened?" She drummed her fingers on the switch and frowned. Pointing a finger at Bella, she started to quarrel at her cat but stopped in mid-harangue when she heard heavy footsteps on her front porch. "Guess who?" she said, becoming accustomed to the sound of Taylor's shuffling walk. "I'll be right with you," she called out.

Although she'd planned to fuss at Bella a bit more, she couldn't do it. She loved Bella too much to make her faithful companion feel as though she'd committed some major crime. Winking at Bella, she said, "I guess I should thank you for solving the mystery of Stephen's not calling." Reasoning that he'd probably been trying for hours, she felt like a weight had been lifted from her heart. There was hope ahead after all--Stephen was honorable, he'd never break his word, of that she was now positive.

She reached for her brief case and favorite fountain pen, the one she'd always used for signing important papers. Relieved that her personal life was still on track, she focused on her job interview. Anxious to explore the options with Taylor's friend, she saw a chance to make a fresh professional start, if the circumstances were right.

Outside on the porch, Taylor bellowed, "Shake a leg, darlin'. It's time to get goin', honey bun." He rapped on her door rudely and rattled the handle impatiently.

Flinging the door open, Anne stood back as Taylor lunged into her living room, red-faced and seeming out of breath.

"I'm ready to go, Taylor, but tell me more about the board meeting at Bellingrath. Who's having it? Someone I know?"

"Didn't I tell you? It's a luncheon for a group of old guard supporters of the Mobile 2001 plan? Just a bunch of civic-minded folks, wantin' to make things better and better. It's good that the corporations they represent fork out lots of dough for the community," Taylor droned as he picked up Anne's overnight bag and ushered her to his car.

Anne frowned and answered, "Of course I know all about that. Livingston Enterprises always went over the top with every fundraising campaign in Mobile, so you really don't need to talk to me about civic responsibility."

"Sorry, dumplin', I didn't mean anything. All I was tryin' to say was that you and I are goin' make an appearance at a stuffy luncheon. But then, we'll split for our road trip-- the Dixie Gambler'd best clear its tables, 'cause, baby, we're on our way." He started his car, gunned the engine, and said with a steely glint in his eye, "Look out world, hear my roar."

Ignoring his comment, Anne tapped on his coat sleeve and said, "Excuse me, Taylor. I thought I was going to interview with your friend this afternoon?"

Taylor zoomed down I-65 to the junction with I-10. Turning right, he soared past a convoy of tractor-trailer rigs and cruised along in the fast lane. "Oh my, Annie, love lips, there was a change of plans. Carson, my pal, couldn't make it this afternoon, so I told him to meet us for dinner in Biloxi. That's all right with you, isn't it?"

Anne smoothed the skirt of her Brooks Brothers suit over her knees and seethed quietly at the schedule change. She'd hoped to have the interview out of the way long before evening. Upset, she said, "If you'd told me earlier, I would've brought along a more suitable evening dress. The one I packed is totally wrong for an interview."

Taylor grinned and shifted into overdrive, careening past a line of cars headed for the Theodore exit.

"Listen, Taylor, I have a solution. After the luncheon, why don't we go back to my house for a minute? I'd really feel much better if I could switch dresses for tonight," she explained, all the while thinking that Stephen might call while she was there.

"Nope, no time for that, prissy puff. Anyway, I want you to wear the pink dress. I like it," he answered as he set his jaw and glared straight ahead.

Distressed that she wouldn't be able to talk to Stephen for hours, she stared out the window, sensing that her phone was ringing at that very moment.

"Almost there, sweet tea," he said, nodding toward a large sign that pointed the way toward the main entrance.

He suddenly blasted his horn at a slow-moving driver and made a fist. "Looks like half of America decided to visit during azalea season," he complained, glowering at the buses, vans, and cars that clogged the narrow entrance road to Bellingrath. He threaded his way through several long lines of cars parked haphazardly by the front entrance and wedged his car into a spot between an Airstream travel van and a tour bus.

"Well, angel eyes, let's get this meetin' in gear, so we can move it on down the road to a night of fun and maybe a few surprises," Taylor said with a wink. He opened the door for Anne and hurried her along the path that wound its way into the manor house that boasted some of Boehm's finest bird sculptures.

"Don't you love these figures?" she asked, adding, "I'd forgotten they were here. I'm afraid I've been so consumed with work that I haven't taken time to enjoy life."

"You poor baby doll, maybe all you've been needin' is a big ol' hunk like me to take care of you. I can give you everything your heart desires, especially in the love department. Come here, sunshine, let this studman give you a preview."

He awkwardly planted a moist kiss on her mouth and tried to open her tight lips with his tongue. When she refused to cooperate, he made a fist and cursed. "Dammit, Anne, what's wrong with you? Last night you had no difficulty opening up for everything I shoved in." With ice in his eyes, he glared at her and turned away, muttering angrily to himself.

Feeling her cheeks redden, Anne swallowed hard and closed her eyes tightly as if to shut out the possibility of her having connected with Taylor in the most intimate way. As she wrung her hands, she tried to think only pure thoughts.

Almost as an answer to her wishes, she heard Taylor say, "Sorry, cream cake, I apologize," his voice dripping with sincerity. Chameleon-like, he changed his dark frown to a sly grin and possessively wrapped his ample arms around her tiny waist. Pushing her along a back corridor that led to a private dining room, he continued to apologize for his rude behavior.

"Okay, Taylor, I forgive you," Anne finally said, wondering why she'd agreed to spend the afternoon and evening with him. She hoped the interview would be worth the effort.

As they entered the dining room, Taylor surveyed the crowd and beamed a bright smile all around. "Some swell digs," he said, as he greeted a banker whose investment group had recently assumed management of Bellingrath Gardens through a trust agreement. He nodded his approval at the noticeable corporate changes that permeated every acre of the beautiful site overlooking Fowl River.

Anne smiled at the men and women who'd gathered around a buffet table ladened with exotic fruits, cajun roast beef, and honey cured ham. Nodding to those she recognized, Anne made her way to the service bar where she selected an iced Perrier. She stood away from the crowd and watched Taylor masterfully work the room with a ready handshake and a beaming smile. Thinking, he's certainly in his own element, she sipped on her drink and smiled pleasantly.

Taylor caught the look of admiration in her eyes and mentally patted himself on the back for another good show. Life was working his way and he liked every moment, especially now that Stephen was back where he belonged, a thousand miles away from Anne.

From the right side of the room, an older gentleman wearing a tan linen sport coat and brown slacks approached Taylor who was glad-handing another man while leering at Anne at the same time. "Taylor, my friend, you seem in awfully good spirits. What's new? Score another deal?"

"Hey, buddy, good to see you," he replied. Then cutting his eyes toward Anne, he said, "As you can see, Lady Luck smiled on me." Winking, he motioned for Anne to join him, but when she didn't come immediately, he yelled, "Hey, pretty puss, I told this ol' rogue I'm datin' a goddess, so get on over here, now."

Anne first shot Taylor a look of exasperation and then decided she should demonstrate tolerance instead of distaste. After all, contact with the right person could mean everything, especially to someone job hunting.

"You dog, you," Taylor's companion replied as he watched Anne walk toward them. "Come on, 'fess up, how'd you land such a pretty lady?"

"Long story," Taylor answered, licking his lips as he watched Anne walk toward him. Reaching for her hands, he said, "I want you to meet someone."

"Honey, what's your name?" Taylor's friend asked, devouring her with his eyes.

Tired of being regarded as an object and no longer caring about making a proper business connection, Anne softly cleared her throat and then roared, "I'm Anne Livingston, former head of Livingston Enterprises, sir, and by the way, Taylor and I are just friends. That's all."

"Oh my, my, what a firecracker! And gorgeous, too, you lucky stiff," the man said as he took one last appraising look at Anne before jovially elbowing Taylor and walking off.

"Now, darlin', don't get all riled up, that guy's just a big kidder," Taylor consoled Anne, although he actually relished the man's approval of his woman.

Brimming with disgust, Anne replied, "I'm sick and tired of being hit on, Taylor. Can't you and your friends see that women hate that kind of attention."

"Ah, ease off, doll baby, you girls like guys who know how to flirt and tease. I know that for a fact," Taylor said with authority. After all, he believed he was the master woman-pleaser, especially since he had yet to be rejected by anyone he'd ever chosen. "And sometimes, surprises come to good little girls, that is, if they mind their manners and do what they should," he added.

Anne shook her head and counted to ten, attempting to prevent another outburst. Knowing that the passion of anger was often a precursor of a stroke, she didn't like to feel her blood pressure spike. The only emotional elevation she wanted to risk was the one that she and Stephen had shared as they'd made their earth spin round and round with every loving glance and touch.

During the time she'd spent with Stephen, she'd felt many emotions that had carried her to the heights of paradise-- and yes, she had to admit to herself, she had enjoyed their mutual flirting and teasing, but that had been different. She didn't feel like a side of prime beef when she was with Stephen; he made her feel special and adored. With Taylor and his friends, who constantly leered and poked at her, she only felt revulsion.

"Didn't you hear me, darlin' dove?" Taylor asked, as he tightened his grasp around her wrist. "You were real good to ol' Taylor last night, so I think you should be rewarded."

Anne shuddered with the fear that she might've made a fool of herself with Taylor and only prayed that Stephen would miraculously reappear in her life and sweep her off her feet and out of Taylor's firm hold. "What are you talking about?" she asked, wanting to put an end to Taylor's innuendoes. If indeed she'd stepped over the line with him, she wanted to know it for sure. All his double talk and knowing looks grated on her nerves and she didn't think she could endure much more.

Taylor pulled her toward his chest and said, "Get ready, angel breath, what I have for you is a surprise. Close your eyes and when I count to three open them wide and watch the door."

He spun her around so that she faced the foyer. Whispering in her ear, he said, "Somebody special is here to see you, babykins. One, two, three, take a look."

Anne gasped as she watched two men walk toward her-- a young one she'd never met and an older man she'd known her whole life.

Unable to contain his glee, Taylor waved to the younger man and shouted out across the room, "Todd, over here."

Anne thought she might faint away. Of all the people she'd expected to see today, the elderly, very distinguished gentleman approaching her was the last on her list.

"Anne, darlin', I've missed our visits so much."

"Oh, granddad. I'm so sorry" were the only words Anne could utter as she felt huge tears welling in her eyes.

Taylor stood back and admired the scene he'd created. Now he had the chance to close the deal with Anne. In just a few hours, he could negotiate his finest coup--all the key players were in place, ready for him to set them into motion.

"Here you go, Todd," Taylor said grimly, stuffing a wad of bills into the man's pocket. "Go buy a new watch--your old one was off by two minutes. Didn't I tell you to have the old man here at 2:30, not 2:32?"

"I'm sorry, sir. I did the best I could but with all the traffic..."

"Excuses don't cut it with me, son," Taylor said, interrupting the young man's explanation. He dismissed him with a curt glare of disapproval. "Next time, follow my orders exactly or you'll be huntin' for another job. Got it?" He sneered as he watched the young man duck his head and sulk away like a whipped dog.

Taylor turned his attention to Anne and her grandfather who'd become the center of attention. Watching a photographer from the Mobile paper snap one picture after another of the pair, he inched closer to Anne and looked at her lovingly.

"Come on over here, son," Bull called out to Taylor. "You need to be in this one, right by your date, my little Annie."

Anne tried to ignore both the matchmaker light that glowed in Bull's brilliant blue eyes and the smirk that stretched across Taylor's face from one large ear to the other.

"See, cuddle kiss," Taylor hissed into her ear, "Didn't I have a wonderful surprise for my true lov.."

"Don't say it, please, Taylor," Anne mouthed silently. Her plate was more than full at the present moment and she struggled to make sense of her situation. She didn't know how to escape the emotional quicksand that seemed ready to swallow her whole. "Help me, help me," she cried silently, praying that some force would rescue her in time.

CHAPTER 12

"Now that wasn't so bad, was it, buttercup? I knew your granddad would understand your troubles," Taylor said as he steered the car with his left hand and patted Anne's knee reassuringly with his right.

Quickly shifting her body weight, Anne squirmed away from his sweaty grasp. "Maybe on the surface he seemed fine, but the sadness in his eyes killed me," she answered softly.

Ignoring her remark, Taylor continued, "Didn't you see how he perked up when I told him I'm gonna trap the rascal who fronted the deal? It all sounds pretty bogus to me-- especially the way your stock soared out of sight but then dipped suddenly. I bet you dinner that's when the snake slipped in the back door and made off with the goods."

"Any idea who's the snake? It wouldn't have been you by any chance?" she asked half-kidding.

Swerving out of a long line of traffic, Taylor brought his car to a quick stop on the shoulder of I-10 just outside the coastal town of Pascagoula, Mississippi. "Now, hang on a minute, doll face, do you honestly think I would do somethin' as underhanded as that to you, my friend from way back when? Not Taylor Hamilton, no way, babe. That's not my style."

Startled by the passion of his words, Anne debated whether she should keep quiet or try to diffuse his huffy mood with an apology. She chose the latter course, saying, "I shouldn't have questioned your integrity. I know you didn't acquire your wealth by devious means because if you had, you wouldn't have a friend around and that's obviously not the case. I saw how everyone at the luncheon listened to your every word. Please, let's forget what I said, okay?"

Taylor grinned broadly as he moved his sleek car back into the line of traffic. His heart warmed to Anne's praise--he liked nothing better than an admiring audience. He glanced at her and smiled, proud of his coup. He'd already profited from the silent acquisition of Anne's company, and now all he needed for a complete victory was to take her, body and soul, into his life. Having watched her mix and mingle successfully in a business/social setting, he knew she was the perfect woman for him.

He no longer worried about her rough edges--those could be honed away as soon as she committed to him. He couldn't wait to recast her into a mold of his ideal. Yes, he thought, all systems are go--she'll soon be mine and mine alone to shape and polish into my dream goddess.

"Did you hear what I said, Taylor?"

"Sure, darlin'. I accept your apology, but I'm no fool. I know somethin' else is on your sweet mind besides your company woes. If you want, you can talk to me about your troubles. Was it that call you made before we left Bellingrath?"

She hated to admit that he was right, but she'd been upset ever since she'd dialed into her answering machine only to find that no messages had been left. Wondering why Stephen hadn't kept his word, she concocted a dozen reasons that would explain why he hadn't called.

Taylor blew off her silence as "woman's moodiness" and babbled on, "After you chat with my pal Carson, I just bet you're gonna have a job offer with a fat salary, then you won't have to worry about that phone of yours ringin'. Please promise that you'll save some time for me."

"Sure," Anne replied, although she had absolutely no intention of continuing her relationship with him. She knew who held her heart in his hands and it wasn't the corpulent fellow sitting beside her.

She tried to put thoughts of Stephen out of her mind and concentrate on the interview ahead of her in Biloxi, but her thoughts kept returning to Stephen. She thought about his muscular body, his chest, his arms, his legs. She shuddered when she remembered how firm he'd felt when he'd held her tightly against him and how their bodies had meshed together perfectly when they'd become one.

Noticing Anne's detachment and the look of wonder on her face, Taylor decided he needed to schedule an appointment for her with a memory specialist. He found her habit of gazing off into space with a dazed smile on her lips most distracting.

That's another personal flaw that's got to go, he thought to himself. I can't have my wife daydreamin' when she oughtta be thinkin' of ways to increase my personal wealth and social standin'. Uncharacteristically subdued by the challenge he saw ahead of him with Anne, he slowed his car at Exit 50 and flipped on the right turn signal.

In silence they passed by glittering casinos stacked like poker chips along the Biloxi-Gulfport beachfront. Suddenly Taylor broke the quiet by yelling, "Dust off your dancin' shoes, suga' button, we've arrived!"

"This is a hotel, Taylor. Why are we stopping here?" She watched him switch off the ignition and then she recoiled at his suggestive smile and his indecent wink that preceded his words, "Be back in a flash, suga' puss."

Afraid she might see someone she knew, she studied the toes of her Ann Taylor pumps and regretted that she'd agreed to this little road trip with Taylor. She chastised herself for allowing the prospects of a job to lure her into unfamiliar territory.

She worried that she'd already made one mistake too many, but maybe her count was slightly off. Taylor was certainly one problem, and a big one at that, but her situation with Stephen was another issue that weighed heavily on her mind.

If Stephen never called her again, the blackmark in the error column beside her name would resemble a huge chunk of coal, making any indiscretion she might've committed with Taylor seem pebble-sized by comparison. Whatever she might've done with Taylor was totally unintentional, but the story with Stephen was different. She'd willingly given herself to him and had savored every moment of the days and the night they'd spent together.

Anne thanked her lucky stars that she hadn't told Stephen of her love for him. She rationalized that if he didn't share her feelings, at least he wouldn't be around to remind her of how deeply she'd fallen for him, head over heels and with no cleats on her naked feet to hold her back.

"I'm such a fool," she sobbed into her tiny closed fist. "How could I've been so stupid? Now all I have is a silent telephone to prove my idiocy."

Just about to break down completely, she stopped weeping when a thought flashed through her subconscious, "Don't give up, Anne Livingston. Why don't you call home one more time?"

"Maybe it's worth a try," she muttered as she spotted a curbside pay station. Bolting from Taylor's car with a quarter and her AT&T calling card clutched tightly in her hand, she gingerly approached the telephone and dialed her number.

She listened to her phone ring and then her outgoing message. By the number of beeps that followed, she could tell that someone had left a message. Almost unable to wait for the tone that commanded her retrieval numbers, she pressed her code, 551, and waited.

"Anne, honey, I've been trying to reach you. I've got some real news about your company that I don't want to give out over the phone. But there's something the whole world can hear--I love you so much that I think I might die."

Stunned, she leaned against the phone booth for a moment. Then, as Stephen's words sank in, she felt her emotions give way. Although almost blinded by her tears of joy, she saw Taylor emerge from the hotel lobby. Running to him, she shouted, "He said he loves me! Taylor, Taylor! Stephen really loves me!"

"Whoa there, missy doll. I don't think ol' Taylor likes the sound of this. After all, I don't believe it's quite proper for the woman I slept with last night to suddenly tell me that some other guy has the hots for her. Somehow that doesn't seem right."

Anne stopped in mid-stride, thinking, surely I didn't sleep with Taylor, that's simply impossible. In a panic, she shook her head and said, "Taylor,...."

"Oh, come here, passion flower, I'll forgive you for leadin' on another man. After all, you hadn't been with me until last night so now that you know who loves you best, you don't have to worry about choosin'." Taylor squeezed Anne's shoulder and added, "Let's bury that dead Richards issue and move on upstairs to our suite. The maids have probably just finished makin' our bed. Bet they left some little mints on our pillows to sweeten our sleep."

"Stop right there, Taylor. I've heard enough," Anne said, incensed by his controlling attitude. "First, I'm not going to share a suite with you, and second, cut out the talk about you and me. It just didn't happen, so drop it, now. I'm not kidding, Taylor Hamilton." She stormed by him as she stalked into the hotel and asked to speak to the manager.

"Fiery lassy, mighty classy," Taylor mocked Anne gruffly. "Have it your way for now, hot lips, but just you wait for my next surprise that has your name engraved on it. Then you'll wanna talk, little Miss Muffet."

Taylor's mind kicked into high gear, furious that Stephen had poisoned his sugar well. Not about to give up, he decided to revise his strategy.

Anne took a pass-key card from the desk clerk and thanked him profusely for finding her a room on the floor below Taylor's suite. Although the hotel had been booked full, a late cancellation had just come across the Telex, allowing her to have a bed away from Taylor's reach as well as some peace of mind. She could see that although Taylor probably meant well, he still could be dangerous if provoked and she didn't feel up to a confrontation.

Not wanting to appear paranoid, she tried to smile at Taylor as he joined her by the front desk. She listened to him bark orders at the hotel staff for a few minutes, but then she closed her ears to his grating voice, choosing instead to let her mind project herself far away from him.

Smiling, she replayed the wonderful moments that she and Stephen had enjoyed when they'd discovered each other's lovespots and had dwelled upon each one until they'd both screamed in pleasure. "Ooh," she said, causing the desk clerk to stare at her warily. Blushing, she looked away.

"Get over here, boy," Taylor yelled to the bellman. Lurching toward him, Taylor snatched Anne's overnight bag out of the man's hands.

Anne shuddered at his rudeness and increased the distance between herself and Taylor.

Sensing her cold reaction, Taylor turned on the charm and became a perfect gentleman as he said, "Follow me, sweetheart." Waiting patiently for her to catch up, he added, "Allow me to hold the elevator for you, princess."

As he watched her walk toward him, he flinched at the dreamy look in her eyes. Suspicious, he frowned, thinking, she's probably gooey-eyed over that overeducated stiff from Rhode Island. Vowing, she belongs to me not him, he clenched his teeth and pictured daggers embedded in Stephen's chest.

"Did you say dinner's at 7?" Anne asked Taylor as the elevator stopped at her floor.

"On the nose, sweet cakes. May I come to your door to escort you on down?" he asked as politely as he could manage.

Demurely, she shook her head and answered, "Umm...better not. Why don't I meet you in the dining room instead?"

"Don't trust yourself with a real man? Is that what you're worried about?" Taylor asked, angry that she seemed determined to go against his wishes. Seeing that she stood fast to her decision, he stared through her and said, "Well, suit yourself, but I'll be waitin'."

"See you then," she said, stepping into the hallway. She breathed a bit easier as she heard the elevator door start to close, but then she heard its warning alarm sound. She turned around quickly. There stood Taylor, licking his lips and leering at her as he blocked the door's closure with one of his puffy hands.

She felt a chill run down her spine when he commanded like a five-star general, "By the way, don't forget to wear the necklace I gave you." With a heavy-lidded wink, he stood back and let the door close.

Anne leaned against a wall, thankful to be alone and away from Taylor's hovering presence. She glanced down the corridor and spotting her room, she ran to her door. Inserting her pass-key, she flung open the door and raced to the telephone on the oak nightstand by the king-sized bed. She hastily dialed Stephen's office number that she'd memorized the moment he'd given it to her.

She listened as the number rang repeatedly, sounding hollow and cold. "Of course, there's no one there," she said. Hanging up, she fussed, "The time zones, that's it, what a difference an hour can make." Disappointed, she put her overnight bag on the foot of the bed and unzipped it slowly, taking out her fancy dress she'd carefully wrapped in tissue paper and her satin shoes.

Wishing that Stephen waited for her downstairs, she prepared instead to meet Taylor's friend, Carson Buckingham III, the man she hoped held the key to her professional rebirth.

Downstairs in the bar, Carson sat statue-like as Taylor prepared him for Anne's interview.

"What about salary, Taylor?"

"Start her at $69,000. That's my favorite number, you know," he said, chuckling into his scotch and soda while he slapped at his fat knees with one of his chunky hands.

Carson grimaced at Taylor's Neanderthal mentality, but didn't cross him, knowing who signed his paychecks. "Heh, heh, right, Taylor," he said, nodding his understanding. "Is that a firm offer?"

Taylor took a long pull on his drink, paused, and furrowed his hairy eyebrows. "Nah, I take it back. She's hungry, so she'll jump at $32,500." Slamming his hands on the top of the bar, he sang, "Hee, hee, hee, that's more money for me."

Carson looked away, seeming uncomfortable by Taylor's outburst.

Taylor reached for a bowl of snacks and popped some nuts in his mouth. Talking with his mouth full, he mumbled, "Before she gets any big money, she needs to learn the ropes starting with chapter one of the Hamilton primer on character judgment." He couldn't fathom her interest in a biological error like Stephen Richards, a man he regarded as a peasant dressed in a suit and tie.

"Is there anything else we should discuss before Ms. Livingston arrives?"

"Nothin' about business," Taylor answered, "but you should throw in that you and I haven't seen each other for years. The less she knows about our dealin's the better. Tonight I want three things to happen--she's gonna walk away employed, she's gonna regret her love for a damn Yankee, and she's gonna wear my ring." Belching rudely, Taylor rose from the bar stool and thumped Carson soundly on the back and said, "Do your part. Got it?"

"Yes sir, Taylor. I can handle this one with my eyes closed," Carson said, smiling knowingly.

"Okay, pal, see you at the table." Taylor shoved his empty tumbler across the bar toward the bartender. "Bring me another one of these to go and total out the tab on the TMK account," he ordered as he stalked off toward the dining room.

Lurking by the main entryway, Taylor cooled his heels as he looked menacingly at his watch--7:05. He didn't like to wait, especially for someone who should feel indebted to him. He ran through his list of good deeds he'd performed on Anne's behalf and concluded he'd been more than fair with her. So what he'd pirated away her company, so what he might have more than a few ulterior motives where she was concerned? Big deal, he determined, reasoning that she wouldn't be hurt in the long run.

Anne spotted Taylor and rushed to his side. "Before you say one word, Taylor, let me talk. I'm sorry I overreacted when we first got here. I know you've only been trying to help me and for that I'm very, very grateful. Please forgive my bad manners. I shouldn't have raved at you like a shrew. You didn't deserve that."

"Well, my goodness, puppy eyes, I certainly didn't expect a greetin' like this. It warms my big heart to hear your sweet words," he said, rubbing his thick fingers along the nape of her neck as he moved her forward to a table set for three.

"Looks like it's show time, Annie, my love. I see Carson waitin' out there so let me rope him on in here. By the way, I like the way my pearl necklace wraps around your throat. And your hair looks good, too, loose and flowin'. Nice, but maybe you oughtta get some gold highlights added next week." As he waved to Carson to join them, he added, "We'll talk about that later, but you'll do for tonight."

"You're just the smartest pants of us all, Annie girl. I watched you charm Carson right out of a job in less than an hour. Good work, darlin'." Taylor pulled Anne next to him and gave her a congratulatory hug. Not satisfied and wanting more contact, he put his hands on her temples. Holding her in an almost vise-like grip, he planted a wet kiss on her trembling lips.

Shaking free from his hold, she took two steps backwards and reached for an after-dinner mint to eradicate his taste from her mouth. She wiped away the moisture he'd sprayed on her face and said, "I'm very pleased with the offer, but I wonder why Mr. Buckingham didn't spend more time evaluating my resume."

"Guess he could see quality from the git-go, suga' plum." Taylor maintained his best poker face, adding, "Thinkin' of figures, you're pretty curvy. Know what, I think you oughtta wear more dresses like the one you've got on. Shows you're all woman."

Embarrassed by his attention, Anne wanted to change the subject. "Look at the time, Taylor. Since we finished our dinner meeting early, we could make it back to Mobile by 11:30, that is if we leave now."

"Oh, no way, sweet toes. Didn't I say that I have more in store for you tonight? So let's go gamble--the night's young and so are we, it's time for us to hit the tables." Taylor pulled a large wad of bills out of his pocket and smiled broadly at his stash. "Burnin' a hole, if you know what I mean."

Anne could see that she couldn't talk him out of a night at the casino so she shrugged her shoulders and accompanied him to the glittering entrance of the Dixie Gambler.

Surrounded by people of all ages and backgrounds, she tried to find a quiet space away from the ringing sound of hundreds of slot machines that players fed non-stop with quarters and silver dollars. She coughed as she swatted at a floating cloud of tobacco smoke and waved off a hostess carrying a full tray of drinks.

Anne glanced at a very ornate clock placed by an escalator and willed its hands to move faster. Resigned to a long evening in a loud place, she hoped the time would pass quickly. All she wanted was to escape back to her hotel room so she could call Stephen--she couldn't wait to tell him about her new job.

Although she knew she had Taylor to thank for the initial contact, she believed that her work stood on its own and she'd received the offer based upon her own merits. She couldn't wait to share her good news with Stephen, the man of her dreams who'd touched her soul like no other.

Get me out of here, she thought, as she listened to someone who'd just lined up three "7's" on one of the machines scream in delight.

Sneaking up behind her, Taylor put his hands around her waist, spun her around, and said, "Look over there, darlin'. There's my ol' friend Jerry." He pointed toward a short, balding man who waved to Taylor as though he'd just been rescued at sea. "Hey, you mud puppy," Taylor called out. "Quit lookin' up the women's skirts, you pervert, and get your ugly puss over here."

The man blushed forty shades of red as people seated at the bar and the slot machines close by stared at him curiously.

Taylor ignored his friend's discomfort and proceeded to kid him unmercifully as he made his way through the crowd. Taking a small package from Jerry's hand, Taylor slapped him on the back and shoved him toward the roulette wheel. "Nice guy for a messenger boy, don't you think?" he asked

Anne who turned up her nose in disdain at Taylor's heavy-handed mannerisms.

"Do you treat all your friends like that?" she asked.

"Like what? Hey, diamond lips, he's a well-paid functionary. You know what I mean, I give him directions and he follows them. That's all. Ol' Taylor doesn't mean anything bad. Get it?"

"Oh yes, Taylor. I see things very clearly," she answered, reaching to loosen her necklace that suddenly seemed to fit too tightly against the slender column of her throat.

"Here, take this roll of dough and go have some fun at the craps table. I've gotta make a phone call and get somethin' ready for you, my little chickadee." Taylor pointed Anne toward a group of people seeming to have a grand time as they placed their bets.

Glad to be away from Taylor, she made a modest wager and waited for the results. Having little luck with the game, she excused herself from the table. Backing away, she accidentally brushed against a large, rather tipsy woman who clung desperately to the drink she carried in her hand.

Not seeing Anne beside her, the woman stumbled and spilled her bourbon and coke down the front of Anne's pink dress. "Oops, sorry," she said with a slur as she tried to mop up the mess with a tiny cocktail napkin.

Reaching for a handkerchief someone had left on an empty table next to where the two women stood, Anne picked it up and dabbed at the front of her dress, saying, "Everything's fine. When I take my dress to..."

Not seeming to hear Anne or not caring what she said, the woman staggered off to rejoin her party and to order another free drink.

Disgusted, Anne wiped at the front of her dress and satisfied that she'd done all she could to save the silk, she folded the bourbon-soaked handkerchief in a neat square.

"What's this?" she asked, looking closely at the linen handkerchief that had a distinctive look and feel to it. She knew she'd seen one like it before, but she couldn't place where. Deciding it wasn't important, she shook her long mane of hair and walked to a picture window that offered a perfect view of Ship Island.

Distracted by raucous laughter coming from a group of men gathered around a roulette wheel, Anne turned to see Taylor standing precariously on top of a wobbly table and waving his fists full of money high in the air. "Over here, doll dimples, look at what I won for you. We're not leavin' now, that's for sure. Why, I should've brought you here sooner, you're my good luck charm, tasty cake."

Taylor blew a kiss to Anne, causing the other players at the wheel to stare at her. Suddenly furious, Taylor warned at the top of his lungs, "Back off from my woman, fellows. She's mine, all mine, so don't get any ideas."

Anne felt much like Taylor's friend, Jerry, chagrined to the core that people associated her with Taylor whose loud and obnoxious behavior bordered on lunacy. Trying to place herself out of his shouting distance, she walked as gracefully as she could through the groups of gamblers that seemed to multiply with each throw of the dice.

Taylor jumped down from his perch and chased after Anne. Breathing heavily, he said, "Quit runnin', little girl, I didn't mean to chase you away. Come on and open the surprise I have for you in my pocket. You'll see how I wanna make up." He spread open his pants pocket and urged Anne to reach inside, saying, "Dig like a miner." He laughed as she looked away while he pushed her hand deep into his pants.

First she felt the cool silk lining of his pocket, but then she touched a small velvety box. Quickly letting go of it as though she'd just touched something vile, she said, "No, Taylor. I don't want it."

"'No's' not a good word for ol' Taylor to hear, candy breath. Here let me help you." He took the jeweler's box out of his pocket and placed it clumsily in Anne's hand that he had to pry open. "This is for you, rosebud. Go on, open it."

Silent, Anne stood in the middle of hundreds, but she suddenly felt very much alone. This was not something she'd anticipated and she didn't quite know how to handle the sticky situation. Taylor had been wonderful in helping her find professional security, but this gift of his was something else entirely. Whatever was in the box she didn't want.

"I said 'open it' and I mean now," Taylor barked, rapidly losing his patience with Anne's reluctance to play by his rules.

Unable to miss the cold glint in Taylor's beady eyes, Anne did as he instructed. "Oh, my gosh!" she exclaimed as she saw a huge diamond set in sparkling gold. "It's absolutely breathtaking, but I can't..."

"'Can't' is another word ol' Taylor doesn't need to hear, lovebug."

"I'm sorry, Taylor, it's the most perfect ring I've ever seen, but I can't accept it," she said, closing the box and handing it to Taylor. "I'm serious, I...." She'd intended to go on, but then she suddenly remembered where she'd seen the linen handkerchief before and who it belonged to.

Thinking, that's Stephen's handkerchief, she felt her soul rock and her heart skip a beat--she knew the love of her life had come to save her. She was sure he was close by, probably watching her and waiting for the right moment to surprise her.

She could barely contain her joy, but her elation soon changed to despair. Hearing laughter, she turned toward the happy sounds and felt her blood run cold. Unable to believe her eyes, she gasped as she watched Stephen, dressed in a Pierre Cardin tuxedo, saunter toward her with a cool blond hanging on his right arm. Clinging to his left side was a very well-endowed, brown-eyed woman who seemed delighted by Anne's distress. Anne felt as though someone had taken her heart and stomped the life out of it.

Taylor's cheshire cat smile spread across his wide face as he whispered into Anne's ear, "Talk about 'Hot Casino Nights!'" Whistling through his teeth, he felt like shaking Stephen's hand. Instead he reached for Anne's hand and asked between maniacal snorts, "Isn't that the man who supposedly loves you dearly?"

Anne threw Taylor a look that could've felled a sequoia and then she glared first at a smiling Marcie MacDonald and then at a positively beaming Brandie Sue. Bristling, she turned her attention to Stephen, who looked panic-stricken. Without giving him a chance to speak, Anne lit into him like a wildcat. "You sorry, sorry man. You're a lying cheat, pure slime. Just who do you think you are? So much for all your talk--you're despicable, a jerk, a phony. Taylor was right about you all along. You're lower than a weasel, a snake, a..."

"Anne, Anne, stop it! Please, I beg you," Stephen pleaded. "Besides, you're not here by yourself."

Ignoring his words, Anne continued her tirade. "I thought you were different and I actually believed that we had a future. How wrong I was. And to think how close I came to telling you that I loved you with everything I have to offer. Such a fool! I should've listened to the person who warned me to stay with my own kind. And that's exactly what I intend to do."

Swinging around to face an amazed Taylor, Anne took the diamond ring from his hand and placed it on her finger. "It's a done deal, Taylor Hamilton. I'm yours, for life."

All color drained from Stephen's face as he broke away from Marcie and Brandie Sue's clutches. Reaching out to Anne, he pleaded, "Please, Anne, stop. Listen for a minute. I can explain..."

Anne wasn't about to wait for any lame excuses, feeling as though she could spit venom like a cobra. She didn't, though. Instead, she took one last look at the threesome whose presence together had changed her life. Locking eyes with Marcie and Brandie Sue, she hissed, "As for you two, I think you're both pathetic. You were pitiful phonies when you whined and connived your way onto the Azalea Maid Court the year I was crowned queen and you're still the same losers today. Take a look at who I'm leaving with and then check out your prize--a man who doesn't know the meaning of the word 'honor.'"

Having a hard time keeping up with Anne as she ran from the casino, Taylor finally matched her stride. Folding her into a huge bear hug, he cooed, "Come on, fairy wings, let's leave those clowns in our dust. The world was made for us and it's about time we started our empire," he said, gloating at his win over the competition and marveling that Stephen had done himself in single-handedly.

Anne shook free from Taylor's hold, realizing that she'd acted before thinking through the consequences. She knew she didn't want Taylor's ring, and she certainly had no intention of marrying him. All she wanted was to escape to the safety of her room.

She forced herself to think of anything except Stephen's betrayal, but her efforts were in vain. Trying hard to maintain her composure, she vowed that she wouldn't shed any tears over the man who'd broken her heart, but she couldn't contain her emotions. Bursting into tears, she sobbed her heart out and she wanted to die.

"Come here, my lady love," Taylor said, as he gathered her petite frame in his burly arms and carried her to his car that the valet had brought to the curb.

"Where are we going, Taylor?" Anne asked, emotionally exhausted.

"To celebrate our engagement I thought we might crack open a bottle of champagne on my boat docked at Bon Secour."

Anne shook her head in disbelief. She hated that she'd created an impossible situation. Just because she'd found Stephen to be as fake as a figure in a wax museum, she shouldn't have fallen over the edge. Now she not only wore Taylor's diamond ring, but she also had to listen to talk of a May wedding to a man she couldn't even bring herself to kiss goodnight. A kiss-off was possible, though, if only she could figure out how to extricate herself from the web she'd spun out of anger, hurt, and disappointment.

In order to get to his cabin cruiser in record time before Anne changed her mind, Taylor took all the shortcuts he remembered from his carousing days when he had a hot date with an early curfew. As his car rapidly ate up the miles, he reassured Anne, saying, "It's all for the best, cream puff. You did the right thing to kick that bum with slicked back hair outta your life. I didn't tell you before but I heard that the skunk who stole your company bore a close resemblance to that buzzard you took a fancy to."

Hearing Anne catch her breath in order to stifle a scream, he knew he was on a roll, so he continued, "You better watch your back around smooth-talkin' creeps like Stephen Richards--they're just no good. Guys like him can't be trusted for a second. Bet he chases women, dumb or ugly, pretty or rich, all day and all night long, always tryin' to score. But he's the real chump if he fell for Brandie Sue's big boobs and Marcie MacDonald's ice maiden routine. I'm not braggin', but I have firsthand knowledge of what those bitchin' babes are all about."

The thought of Stephen becoming involved with either woman turned Anne's stomach. Her imagination took over at that point and tormented her with graphic scenes of Stephen entwined first with Marcie and then almost suffocated by Brandie Sue's cleavage. Holding back sobs and tears, she attempted to regain control.

"Taylor, this isn't right. I don't care what happens to Stephen, Marcie, or Brandie Sue, but I do care about us. So much so that we have to stop this charade right now. I'm sorry but I can't marry you and if I carry this pretense any further, I will be as much a liar and a cheat as Stephen Richards."

She removed Taylor's diamond ring and reached across the gearshift to place it in his coat pocket. "I'm really sorry but I can't go through with this. Please take me home."

Incensed, Taylor felt something snap inside of him. "You lyin' witch. If you think I'm givin' you back to him then you've got another thing comin'. I'll show you who wears the pants in our family and babe, believe me, it's not you."

Anne held her breath as Taylor swerved the car toward the right and headed down a bumpy, unmarked country lane that led to the cold bay waters. She closed her eyes and prayed for strength to fight off a man more than twice her size. When she looked to the heavens, instead of stars she only saw dark clouds and streaks of lightening flash across the sky. Brokenhearted and frightened, she willed herself to survive, regardless of the odds stacked against her.

The car roared to a sudden stop, giving Anne only a few seconds to escape. She tried to open her door but she stopped when she felt a cold piece of steel press against her left temple.

"You'd better pray harder, Anniepoo. I mean business, love child--if I can't have you, nobody can," Taylor said with a growl as he half-dragged, half-pushed her out of his car and onto the dock where a cabin cruiser waited for a wild ride toward the churning Gulf of Mexico.

CHAPTER 13

Anne felt her heart leap to her throat as the boat's twin engines ignited with a surge. She held on for dear life not knowing whether she should try to escape or hope Taylor's anger would subside. She struggled to remember the strategies she'd learned in her classes that dealt with terrorism in the business world, but riddled with fright, she couldn't even recall her professor's name.

"Hey, boy, didn't I tell you to watch that throttle? This isn't a new model, you know," Taylor called to the mate who'd met them on the dock in the middle of the night. "What a blockhead--probably can't tell the ignition from the loran and lousy at tellin' time, too," he muttered as he tested the ropes he'd tied securely around Anne's wrists.

"Sorry, sir," the mate mumbled as he worked the cruiser's controls.

"Speak up, idiot, that is, if you have somethin' worthwhile to say," Taylor snarled back.

"Please, Taylor, listen to me for a minute. We can work out our differences," Anne begged, holding back her tears of fear that threatened to flow at any moment.

"Shut up, Ms. Livingston, you've already talked more than enough. As for workin' somethin' out, believe me that I have every intention of puttin' you to work on your back before I toss you overboard for the shark's early mornin' feed."

Anne closed her eyes tightly, remembering the tragedy in the Gulf that'd claimed the lives of her loved ones. She wondered about the condition of the water now. Would it be as still as a lake or rough and rolling? Fearing the worst, she knew she should devise a survival plan, but she drew a blank on what she should do as she faced her own emergency at sea. Crying, "Stephen, Stephen," she regretted the way they'd parted and wished she could roll back time.

"Moanin' about fancy boy? Don't you understand that he doesn't care about you and never did? Are you that blind to the truth?" Taylor asked, sneering at her.

"I don't understand why you're doing this to me," Anne replied, hoping he might come to his senses before it was too late.

Irately, Taylor cackled and yelled over the roar of the boat's engines, "You tramp, you're dumb as a dodo if you can't figure out what you did wrong. You shouldn't have turned ol' Taylor down, but since you did, you're gonna have to pay the price."

Anne shivered, both from the harshness of his words and from the cold salt spray that hit the side of the boat as they flew across the back bays. Having sailed over the same waters many times before, she mentally plotted their course.

"Answer me, you useless twit," Taylor screamed into Anne's face. "Why him and not me?"

Trying to recall the meditation techniques that'd aided her in tight spots before, she centered herself and answered, "I guess it doesn't matter now, so, Taylor, I'll tell you the truth. I chose Stephen Richards because he was everything and more that I'd ever hoped to find in a man. I really loved him, I still do."

Taylor strode menacingly toward Anne and placed his hands firmly around her throat. "I should choke the life out of you right now, but I won't because you owe me somethin' and I want that dessert served up at sea."

Suddenly the boat shifted directions, throwing Taylor off balance and away from Anne. She breathed a deep sigh of relief at her narrow escape and prayed that Taylor had hit his head when he'd fallen backwards.

Cursing a blue streak, Taylor climbed to his feet and charged at the mate in the cabin, shouting, "What are you tryin' to do, kill me? If you don't watch your step, you *#@! clod, you'll go overboard the same way as our honored guest."

Anne closed her ears to Taylor's rantings that spewed from the control room and concentrated instead on her local geography. The lightning bolts that illuminated the dark, raging sky helped her gather her bearings. She thought she recognized the shoreline around St. Andrew's Bay, so she figured they were approaching Navy Cove and the Sunset Bay Marina. Wanting to flash a distress signal, she looked around for a light or a reflector, but nothing of that nature was within her reach.

She felt the boat rock and sway with every wave that pushed against its creaking hull. Glad for a steady sea stomach, she moved in sync with the pounding water. That's it, she thought, as she took advantage of the back and forth motion of the boat. Rubbing her bound wrists against the edge of an ice bucket filled with champagne, she worked to loosen the rope ties.

She thought about life, its ups and downs, its highs and lows. "Mine's about over," she said, "but I'm not going to go out dwelling on the negative." She closed her eyes and willed herself to think of the happiest time in her life.

Into her mind flashed memories of the night of miraculous love she'd spent with Stephen when they'd surrendered themselves to the eternal dance of the waves. With every crest and fall, she'd sworn that lovemaking couldn't get any better. And each time Stephen had proved her wrong by taking her repeatedly to the stars and back to earth again. The sand had cushioned their bodies and the soft breezes from the Gulf had cooled their fevered brows when they'd come up for air--two lovers on the dunes, paradise found. Oh, what she would give for just one more time with Stephen.

She tried to dismiss her longing for his kisses that'd caused fire to rage deep inside her tenderest spot. Even though she knew she shouldn't desire someone who'd betrayed her, Anne couldn't forget him. She'd told Taylor the truth--she loved Stephen and she always would, regardless.

Anne snapped back to the present when she felt a change in the boat's movement as it entered waters that ran deeper and rougher than those of the bays. Although darkness surrounded the shaky craft, she could tell by the dim, flickering lights on shore that they were rounding the Point and passing by Fort Morgan where Confederate soldiers had blasted cannon fire at Union warships. She regretted not showing Stephen the casements that remained there. She knew he would've appreciated the historical value of the place and its haunting beauty.

Her eyes filled with tears. She wished she could take back the hurtful words she'd spoken to Stephen at the casino. She hated that she'd been so quick to rush to judgment without allowing him a moment to explain. Closing her eyes, she prayed for a chance to make things right.

Suddenly tossed forward, Anne heard a roar and a crash and a blood-curdling scream. She knew that the boat had hit something solid and was breaking apart. As tears streamed from her eyes, she prepared for her end, offering up a silent prayer for Stephen to find someone who could make him happy.

Then an overpowering surge of water crashed against her, snapping Taylor's ropes free from her wrists and allowing her some buoyancy against the cold waves that pulled toward the shore. Feeling empowered by a burst of strength and her will to live, Anne swam parallel to the currents and rode the top of the powerful whitecaps to safety.

Disoriented and wearing only fragments of her soaked evening dress, she crawled on the beach, not caring if she bumped into a Portuguese man-of-war or a sea serpent. She believed that after all she'd been through, she could face the slimiest creature the Gulf could spit out--nothing could be as horrifying as the cruel beast named Taylor Hamilton.

Anne felt the salt water burn her eyes as she squinted, trying to figure out where she'd made landfall. Then she laughed, thinking, it doesn't really matter, I'm safe, out of harm's way. She tried to stand up, but her rubbery legs caved in, dumping her into the wet, mushy sand. Undaunted, she decided to crawl to shelter somewhere to wait out the storm that threatened to unleash its fury at any moment.

"Where are you goin', angel fish?" a man asked from his perch above Anne on a shadow-covered high dune.

Anne screamed, "Oh, no, not you!"

"Just ol' Taylor. Here to service your every need, pussy foot." He lunged toward her, snarling and snorting like a wild animal.

Anne winced at the sound of his throaty chuckle that echoed along the deserted beach. Refusing to allow him near her, she averted his advances and swore, "You'll have to kill me first."

Crazed with desire and hatred for the woman who'd refused his demands, Taylor ripped open a waterproof pouch he'd salvaged from the boat. He pulled out a .38 caliber revolver and laughed. As a flash of lightning lit up the sky and glimmered on his blue steeled gun, he pointed it toward Anne and said, "Suit yourself and know you just gave your last executive order." With a sneer flickering across his face, he staggered closer to Anne who'd collapsed at his feet.

Aiming at her head, he moved in for the kill.

Anne heard the shot go off and she fainted at the sound.

CHAPTER 14

When Anne came to, she thought she must've become an angel. Her heart felt so light, free of all cares--she'd never felt safer. Then she realized that she wasn't alone. She snuggled into a pair of strong arms that held her closely, imparting the love she'd thought she'd never feel again. She closed her eyes and opened her heart as she accepted a tender kiss that tasted like wine.

"Hello, gorgeous."

"Oh my goodness!" she called as tears streamed down her cheeks.

"Don't cry, precious. The storm's passed, you're safe now, and no one will ever hurt you again. I'll stay by your side for eternity--that is, if you'll let me."

Widely opening her eyes, she took in all of Stephen's compelling masculinity. In his fight for survival against the storm, he'd lost most of his clothing, except for his silk boxers that strained with his magnificent manhood.

Anne shook her hair that was matted with seaweed and windblown out of control. Feeling the damp sand beneath her, she rejoiced that she was still on earth and not sitting on a cloud. "Stephen, is it really you? No, I must be dead and dreaming. The last time I saw you we were in Biloxi and you weren't with me."

"And that's where you're wrong, Anne." Then he bent toward her, gently kissing the tip of her nose and her eyelids.

"Wait a minute, I'm not following you. I saw you with Marcie and Brandie Sue, cuddling like puppies in a manger," she said, pulling away from him just enough to show her displeasure but not far enough to stop him from reaching for her inner thighs.

"Oh, but I was with you, not them."

Anne rolled her eyes and laughed.

"No, Anne, I'm serious. I was really acting on your behalf. It was all a ruse to get the lowdown on that rat Taylor Hamilton. I just took a page out of his book and used one of his tricks. I know you won't approve, but I decided the best way to find out everything about him was through women he'd used and discarded," Stephen explained.

"You mean Marcie and Brandie Sue?"

"Both of them sang like canaries after a couple of bottles of wine and..."

"Spare me the details," Anne replied. "But when did you contact them?"

Stephen sighed, wanting to put the past behind them so they could move forward to a life of love.

"Well?" she prodded.

"My plane had a fog delay in Atlanta so I used the time to do some investigating on my own about your company and Taylor's corporate games. You know, a funny thing about takeovers is that there's usually a weak link somewhere. In your case, it was Bruce Floyd, your V.P. for Finance. He was a man on the move with a major cash flow problem."

"Oh, Stephen, surely not Bruce. You've got to be mistaken." Anne found it hard to believe that someone she'd known for years as a loyal friend could've turned against her.

"Sorry, Anne. He leaked your every plan and financial transaction to the highest bidder."

"Name names. Who was it?" she asked, although she had a pretty good idea.

Stephen kissed her deeply. Then he asked, "Wouldn't you rather play hide and seek with me for a while instead of bothering with this business chatter, my love?"

"It was Taylor, wasn't it?"

Outlining her lips with his tongue, Stephen stopped only to nod his head. Then he continued his very personal examination of Anne's luscious body.

Not ready to give in totally, she playfully pushed him backwards and said, "Confess it all, mister, or there's no more peek-a-boo play for you. How did you know that I had a gambling date with Taylor?"

"Let's say that he bragged one time too many. When I uncovered his shady exchange of cash for information that led to the theft of your company, I returned on the next plane to Mobile. During the flight, I reached Brandie Sue by airphone--she knew all about where Taylor planned to take you, the set-up interview, and the bogus job offer that was intended to entice you into permanent servitude. She told me everything and even offered to enlist Marcie's help in driving me to Biloxi."

Anne thought of her sorority sisters who'd ended up disliking Taylor after only a few encounters. Now she had personal knowledge of why they'd run from him. "Taylor must've hurt Marcie and Brandie Sue before. Is that why they turned against him?"

"Yes and well, I'm not sure how to put this," he drawled slowly, "but I think they thought they might have their way with me as a bonus."

Anne pinned Stephen's tall, willing frame to the ground and held him securely with her small fingers wrapped through his sopping wet, but still soft hair. "Did they?" she demanded.

Stephen smiled and laughed, "Of course not. I'm a virtuous man at heart." And then he gently flipped Anne over and matched his body to hers, length to length, man to woman, lover to lover.

The sun began to rise but Stephen and Anne were too preoccupied with one another to notice the first light of dawn. Only the beguiling call of a lonely gull made them aware that they were not alone on the beautiful beach by the now calm emerald waters.

Lazily stretching, Anne raised up on her elbows and looked at Stephen whose love shone back at her through his deep eyes. "I still don't know how we got here together."

"Brandie Sue called a friend who's a helicopter pilot stationed at Keesler in Biloxi. I'm sure he's still all smiles from the reward she promised him for airlifting me to the dock ahead of you and Taylor. But I was almost too late."

"How so?"

"I had about two minutes to neutralize your trusted colleague Bruce Floyd before you and Taylor arrived dockside."

"What?" Anne couldn't believe what she was hearing.

"Yes, Taylor had confided in Brandie Sue that your ex-VP was supposed to be Taylor's mate on his loveboat. Thank goodness Bruce has a cowardly streak as wide as an airfield because when I got to him first and told him Taylor had turned ugly, he wanted out. That's when we traded clothes and I ended up wearing his rubber suit, boots, and goggles and off we went."

Amazed, Anne sighed and said, "That explains the bumpy ride, especially when Taylor got too close to me. Right?" She knew that Stephen had risked his life to save hers.

"Hey, beautiful. Unlike you, I didn't spend my youth at the Yacht Club or attend sailing camps in the summertime. My ride may've rocked and rolled more than a pro's, but some of the words I heard come out of your precious lips made the journey lots smoother for me--especially your confession about loving me, regardless." His eyes twinkled with glee when he watched Anne blush as only a lady can.

"Okay, that's enough teasing. Seriously, we need to talk about Taylor. What happened?"

Stephen became very still. "He's alive--he took a bullet in the shoulder that only winged him. When I crept up behind him and knocked the gun away from your direction, I honestly didn't know what would happen. You were my only concern."

"Oh, Stephen, you saved my life." Holding Stephen's bloody and bruised hands, Anne knew he'd been in a fight, but sensing that he didn't want to talk about it, she didn't press for more details.

Stephen shook his head, remembering how he'd pulverized Taylor with one blow to the side of the beast's obtuse head. Blotting it from his mind, he turned his attention to Anne.

"Correction, Anne. I saved 'our' life for without you I would be nothing." Not giving her a chance to speak, he kissed her tenderly and whispered in her ear, "I love you with all my heart and soul."

"You love me?" she asked dreamily.

"Yes, darling, I do, I honestly do. No one will ever come between us again."

"Taylor? Where is he?"

"Probably sleeping it off in the...what county is this?"

"Baldwin," Anne answered.

"...in the Baldwin County jail. He's got a long rap sheet to face and the feds will be after both Taylor and Bruce for their dirty tricks. But Anne, my darling, enough of this. I have a question for you. Will you marry me and be mine forever?"

Feeling a lump rise in her throat and tears flood her eyes, she bowed her head and answered softly, "Oh, Stephen, yes, yes, I'll marry you. I love you so much."

Stephen held Anne for a long time before he trusted his words. "And I'll love you forever."

With pelicans and sea gulls circling overhead and the sands shifting beneath them, they reaffirmed their lasting love for one another on the fiery dunes that basked in the rays of the morning sun.

EPILOGUE

Ten Years Later

"Bay View"

Point Clear, Alabama

The children napped quietly upstairs in their rooms decorated with bunnies and chicks while their parents billed and cooed in the double jacuzzi that faced Mobile Bay. Tickling Anne's nose with soft pink bubbles propelled by the strategically placed jets that lined the marble spa, Stephen drew Anne against his chest and said, "You're as beautiful today as ten years ago when we shipwrecked on the beach at Fort Morgan. I loved you then with all my heart and my feelings for you haven't diminished one iota."

"Oh, Stephen, the things you say. It's no wonder I fell for you," Anne replied, softly soaping the area of his body that responded to her every loving touch.

Relaxing against a shell-shaped headrest, he smiled with the look of contentment that only develops over time. "We really made a pair then, two beachcombers washed up by the wind and the water."

Laughing at the memory, Anne took a sip of chilled wine and shared a long and luxurious kiss with the man of her dreams and the love of her life. "I'm surprised our neighbors at the beach didn't call the sheriff when we appeared at their door. We looked so frightful."

"Oh, I don't think so," Stephen disagreed teasingly. "We just appeared totally satiated--head over heels in love."

Anne smiled, thinking about how far she and Stephen had come together, through the good times and the bad, the happy, the sad. "We have so much to be thankful for-- our Jessica and Jimmy, our beautiful home, and our love for each other."

"Don't forget the growth of Livingston & Richards, Inc. Did you see this morning's NASDAQ report? Our stock's shooting the lights out of the competition," Stephen said proudly as he caressed Anne's still perfect, creamy thighs.

Stephen looked into her radiant blue eyes and said, "I'll always remember that fateful night when I caught the return flight to Mobile from Atlanta, blowing off my career in Providence. It's a darn good thing that you held no gender biases when you offered me a job after the SEC returned control of your company to you."

"Hey, handsome, I had to make an honest man of you. Besides, I enjoyed faxing in your resignation," she teased, bending lower and lower to taste his divine sweetness.

"Better stop, darling, because I'm about to challenge NASA's Discovery for its position in orbit." His eyes sparkled with adoration when he added, "You are the siren of the sea--just looking at you drives me out of control. And when we kiss, my heart grows..."

"And that's not all, my dear husband. Tell me more."

Stephen held Anne's left hand and admired the simple gold band she wore. "Don't you think it's about time you let me get you a diamond to go with this?"

"No darling, our wedding ring says everything that's important. Eternity. Having your love is all that I need and all I'll ever want," she answered quietly as sweet tears welled in her eyes.

Kissing her softly, Stephen gathered her in his arms, lifted her out of the warm swirling water, and gently carried her to their bed of love.

To order additional copies of **Fiery Dunes**, complete the information below.

Ship to: (please print)

Name _____

Address _____

City, State, Zip _____

Day phone _____

_____ copies of *Fiery Dunes* @ $8.95 each $_____

Postage and handling @ $2.50 per book $ _____

Tax (Alabama residents only) @ $0.36 per book $ _____

Total amount enclosed $ _____

Make checks payable to *Lorelei Publications*

Send to: **Lorelei Publications**
P.O. Box 3774 • Gulf Shores, AL 36547-3774

To order additional copies of **Fiery Dunes**, complete the information below.

Ship to: (please print)

Name _____

Address _____

City, State, Zip _____

Day phone _____

_____ copies of *Fiery Dunes* @ $8.95 each $_____

Postage and handling @ $2.50 per book $ _____

Tax (Alabama residents only) @ $0.36 per book $ _____

Total amount enclosed $ _____

Make checks payable to *Lorelei Publications*

Send to: **Lorelei Publications**
P.O. Box 3774 • Gulf Shores, AL 36547-3774